Guts Vs. Glory

By Jason B Osoff

W9-AOB-494

To my friends and family for all their support and encouragement. I could have done it without you, but it would have been awfully hard.

Prologue

As an athlete, you tend to remember important games throughout your career. You remember your first game in high school, in college, and, if your lucky, the pros. You remember the game you broke records, the game you were part of a championship team, and even your first big defeat. However, as the father of an athlete, every game your child plays in is memorable. I knew, as I watched my son play his first game as a third grader, that it would be one of the many games I would never forget. Even though his team lost, he was smiling from ear to ear the entire time. He reminded me of my times at East Whitaker and how much fun he and I had.

The High School Years

Chapter 1

I first met Michael Upton in Kindergarten. We knew we were meant to be best friends because he was the smallest kid in our class, while I was the biggest. The best part of our friendship was that we never had to impress each other, or do stupid things to get the other's attention. We were able to be who we were, without ever worrying about what the other person thought. It was different when it came to others, though.

Going into our junior year of high school, we spent most of our summer nights roaming the streets of downtown Whitaker. We never broke any laws, and we always came home on time, so our parents never asked what we were up to. However, one night we were approached by some our classmates. They pointed to a car parked on the side of the road that had its windows down. They thought it would be funny to grab and hide the laptop sitting on the front seat. As we were thinking about joining in, someone mentioned that it wouldn't be a crime because the windows were down. Since it was only a harmless prank, we were going to play along; we knew it wouldn't hurt to have some more friends going into 11th grade. All we needed to do was grab the computer, then hide it somewhere else in the car. Mike decided that he would grab the backpack in the back of the car so that he had something to do. Both windows were down, so we walked over to the car, reached in, grabbed the items, took them out of the car, and, as our hearts stopped simultaneously, dropped them at our feet.

The other guys must have seen the cops because as we made eye contact with the Becker County deputies, our new friends were nowhere to be found. As soon as the officers told us to freeze, I was done. I was the biggest kid in my class, so running was not my forte. Honestly, I don't remember ever running as a kid. I was even nice enough to voluntarily lie down on my stomach with my hands behind my back so the officer could quickly restrain me. Not Mike, though. He ran. He was fast and made it really far. Until that time, I had never seen someone run so fast. And as impressed as I was with his running, I was even more impressed with the tackle.

Out of nowhere, a Becker County deputy, standing at nearly seven feet tall, and weighing easily over 300 pounds, stood right in his path. In that instant, it was speed versus strength. As soon as they made contact, Mike's forward momentum stopped and he was quickly taken to the ground. Strength won. The deputy never ran after him, he just used his body size to his advantage and stopped him dead in his tracks, taking him hard to the ground.

If we were to plan that night out differently, we should've looked out for anyone watching us. Also, running away, towards the police station, probably wasn't our best idea; then again we never were the smartest kids. Personally, I don't regret a single thing. That was the night that changed our lives forever.

Chapter 2

We were literally right around the corner from the Becker County jail, so the ride in the plastic coated back seat was quick. While in the car, Mike asked me why I was grinning and if I realized that we were going to jail for what we did. I told him that if he had seen the officer's tackle, he would be grinning too. Mike pointed out that he was still faster than the other cops who were chasing after him, which then made him smile too.

Upon our arrival, we were escorted to the police desk by the deputies. There, our fingerprints and pictures were taken. The big officer was curious why I was smiling for my mugshot. I told him that all I could think about was his hit. My smile quickly vanished, though, when he informed us that we were both being charged with felonies. Apparently, the car we were messing with belonged to the Becker County Sheriff's Department, and was being used for sting operations. Apparently it was a crime to take items from a car, even when the windows were wide open. The news got even worse when he told us that our parents were on the way to post our bail.

I wasn't afraid of what my parents would say to me. I was relieved that I wouldn't be sitting in a jail cell overnight, and I knew that I deserved whatever punishment my parents decided to pile on. What hurt was the fact that my parents were always there for me, but I still ended up disappointing them. They tried their hardest to raise a good kid, but as hard as they tried, they still had to pick up that good kid from jail. I've done bad things in my life before, but this was the first time the police had to get involved.

Our parents all arrived at the same time. As they walked in, no eye contact was made and no words were exchanged. The only words spoken in those few minutes were those of the deputy explaining why we were there and what the punishment could be. Soon, we were on our way home. My mom spent the entire ride telling me how disappointed and upset she was at me. She thought that she had raised me better than to steal stuff just to impress some kids from school. As bad as I felt, I was more afraid of my dad's reaction. As my mom was yelling at me, he didn't say a word. I know his wrath would come soon... but when?

Finally, after she was done, it was my dad's turn. He produced the real yelling I was expecting. My dad wasn't much for yelling, so I knew I messed up really bad. A few minutes later, my parents had even more bad news for me. My parents said that they weren't going to punish me for what I did; which sounded great until they added that they would instead stand behind whatever punishment the judge had for me. A week before the school year, we would have to go to court for the crimes we committed, with the real possibility of a long prison sentence.

That night, I hardly slept. Every time I closed my eyes, I imagined what my life would be like as a prisoner. Whenever I opened my eyes, I felt my room caving in and imagined what living in a jail cell would feel like. Then I thought about my life after prison. I wouldn't have a high school diploma, so I wouldn't be able to find a job. I saw myself as a 30 year old, living in my parents' basement, selling magazine subscriptions door-to-door. I wasn't the best kid, but I knew my life had more potential than that.

Chapter 3

We weren't the best of students; how we made it to the 11th grade without repeating a year was a surprise even to us. Simply put, we didn't like school. We always felt that we had better things to do. School, however, would be a blessing compared to the option of spending time behind bars.

Court was very intimidating. The judge looked massive as he was sitting behind his giant desk. To make matters worse, his desk was elevated so that he would have to look down on us as he spoke. When he talked, he let us know how serious of an environment his court room was, and made us realize that he would be taking this trial very seriously.

The judge told us that he read the police report, as well as our statements. He understood that we took the items out of the car due to peer-pressure, and had no intention of stealing the items. However, the fact remained that we took items out of a car on our own free-will. Since the items had a value of over $1,000, the judge could easily charge us both with felonious larceny from an automobile. The maximum sentence could be up to five years in prison, in addition to a $10,000 fine.

After the judge gave us a few minutes to sweat it out, his tone changed. He knew that neither one of us had a criminal record, and he accepted the fact that we were simply dumb high school kids who gave in to peer-pressure *way* too easily. He decided that he wasn't going to charge us with a felony, but at the same time he couldn't just let us go unpunished. To keep us off the streets at night, the judge made us join an after-school program. We were required to attend the program on a daily basis, and would not be allowed to show up late. If we didn't fulfill those simple requirements, we would be sent to jail for two years.

It seemed like a good deal at the time. Rather than going to jail and ruining our lives, we were given a second chance. But then it dawned on us; the school that we hated so much would be our new prison. Rather than leaving at 2:30 with the rest of the students, or being able to skip school at least once a month, we were required to stay after school every day. To make matters worse, it wasn't a simple hang out in the gym for a couple of hours; we were required to join an activity that we weren't familiar with, and work with students that we probably didn't like.

Not only would our school be our new prison, but the teachers would be our wardens; required to report our every move to the judge. The other students would become our prison guards, making our lives a living hell as they no doubt enjoyed their after-school programs, embarrassing us because we would look like fools compared to them. Jail was quickly sounding like a better option.

Chapter 4

A week later, our sentence was set to begin as the first day of school was upon us. That day, students would be allowed to sign up for an after school program. The auditorium was full of eight-foot long tables, each decorated and labeled for the club they represented. We didn't know where to begin, so we started with the table closest to the entrance.

The first table was the band program. We listened to rap and heavy metal music all the time, and being able to start our own band sounded kind of fun, so we figured we could give them a try. We were even willing to learn how to play the drums or the guitar. We were ready to sign up until the representative at the table started talking. That person had "band nerd" written all over him. Apparently, East Whitaker was known for their marching band. In fact, they had more people in the band than their entire senior class. That club was clearly for band nerds who couldn't get enough of the french horn or tuba, and wanted to spend time with other band nerds. Those nerds had been playing their instruments since the 5th grade, and could out-clarinet us any day. Next.

The next table was the honor society. That group consisted of students that really liked school and had really good grades. Next.

We skipped the chess club, the key club, and the math club, but we stopped at the drama club. That was another club where we thought we knew what we were getting into. We loved movies, and we thought acting would be fun. Just like before, we were ready to sign up until the representative told us about her group. Memorizing lines and acting like someone else in front of an audience would've been a challenge, but something that we could've overcome. What we wouldn't be able to overcome was the fact that we would be performing in plays where we would be wearing make-up, singing, dancing, and making complete fools of ourselves. Next.

But there was no next. We were out of options, so we took a walk outside. We decided that our only talents were Mike's running abilities and my size. Unfortunately, those talents would be wasted in drama, chess, or band. I thought back to the big deputy and how he was able to use his size to his advantage without needing to be fast or athletic. Why couldn't I do the same with my size? Then we saw them. Out on the field, with their dark purple helmets glimmering in the sun, the varsity football team was running, catching, tackling, and blocking. That's when it came to us: the football team met after school, which would fulfill the after-school aspect of our sentence, while the field would be the best place to use our natural talents. Then, for the first time I could remember, I ran. We both ran - straight to the coach to sign up for the school's football team.

Chapter 5

We soon realized that the football team was not like any of the after-school clubs in the gym. There was no table to sign up at, and no advertisements for future members. It was a group that had spent the entire summer practicing together, and was not interested in recruiting new members. Unfortunately, we didn't realize that until after the coach stopped laughing at us when we asked about signing up.

Once he stopped laughing, he told us that he would talk to us after practice. In the meantime, we were invited to stay and watch. At first, we were very intimidated. Clearly, this group had already become a solid team. They knew the drills and had already begun working on plays. Even more intimidating was the level of skill that those players had. I was watching the runners, knowing I could never compete at their level. They were running fast, they were running hard, and they were even running backwards. Mike was watching the tacklers. They were knocking the tackling dummies into the next field. As a runner, he was scared by the amount of force those tacklers had to give.

After a few minutes, however, our attentions switched and we were suddenly enjoying ourselves. I began watching the tacklers, while Mike watched the runners. He knew he was faster than most of the guys out there, even though he didn't know any of the plays. I knew I wasn't ready for what the tacklers were doing, but I was more than willing to learn. The more I watched them, the more I wanted to hit somebody.

After practice, the coach sat us down in his office. After explaining our situation to him, the coach said that he would be willing to ask the judge if the football team could be considered an acceptable after-school program. He then explained that we would be faced with the challenge of learning the team's plays quickly because the first game of the season was scheduled at the end of the week. His biggest concern was that because we missed the first two weeks of practice, which were aimed at getting the team in good shape, he didn't know what kind of shape we would be in. He decided that he would attempt to assess our athletic ability during gym class the following day. Since the coach was also the gym teacher, he would be able to pull us out of class to assess our speed and strength. From there, he would know how far behind we were, and what we would need to do to catch up to the rest of the team.

We were excited that the coach was giving us a chance. Rather than turning us down right away, he was willing to take time out of his day to see if we had any potential. It would then be up to us to prove our dedication to the team, as well as our willingness to stay committed to the program. Suddenly, our excitement turned to shock. As we were shaking hands with the head coach of the varsity football team, he referred to us as *his* players. The next day wasn't a tryout, we already made the team.

Chapter 6

We were not forgotten about. Just like he told us he would, the coach pulled us aside from the other students during gym class. It was the second day of class, so we weren't really missing much anyway. While the other students were playing flag football, we had a private meeting with the coach on the other end of the football field. He began the meeting by informing us that, although it was a stretch, the judge would consider football an after-school program. The coach then told us that he wanted to do a quick assessment of us to see what we would need to improve on. He was most concerned with our speed and strength.

The first thing he had us do was stand at one end of the flag football field. We were instructed to run as fast as we could for 20 yards. Clearly, Mike had no problem with that, but when I was done, I couldn't breathe. Without even getting a chance to catch my breath, it was time for the second drill. We started at the same place as before, but this time, we ran to the 10-yard line, turned back around and ran back to the starting line, then turned back around and ran to the 20-yard line. The back and forth running continued until we finished at the 50-yard line. We ended up running 250 yards during that drill. I think I'm still trying to catch my breath. But like before, that was a drill made for Mike.

After the speed drills, we were ready to move on to the strength drills. The first drill was to see how many pushups we could do in a minute. After numerous attempts, we were finally able to do a perfect push up. Unfortunately, we were only able to do *one* perfect pushup. Next were the sit-ups. We struggled to figure out the right form for those too, but eventually we were able to complete 10 of them. Our last drill was squats. For that drill, we had to squat down as far as we could without bending our back, then come back up with our knees locked. After the fifth one, neither of us could get back up.

With the drills finally done, we clearly didn't need the coach to tell us what we needed to work on. I needed to work on my speed, while we both needed to work on our strength. The coach did tell us, though, that he was impressed with Mike's natural speed and felt that if I got stronger, I could defiantly use my large size to my advantage. He promised us success by the end of the season if we stuck with his workout plan. We quickly committed to his plan, but our level of commitment decreased the more the coach described what his workout plan entailed.

Since I would play as a lineman, the coach wasn't too worried about my speed. He told me that I would get faster once I maintained a healthy diet and increased my cardio. Unfortunately, we couldn't do our individual work during practice, and we couldn't keep missing gym class. That left us with only the time before school to use the school's weight lifting room. With a school day that started at 7:30, our sessions would have to start at 6am. For students going to bed after midnight, 6am seemed like a nightmare. To stay on the football team, we would have to go to bed early, wake up early, get to the gym early, push ourselves lift weights and run on the treadmill, stay in school all day, then finish with a three hour practice. To make matters worse, the coach said that we would have to raise our grade point average to stay on the team. That meant that we would have to do our homework in the limited time between the end of practice and going to bed early. Suddenly, what should've been a fun activity of running and hitting people, was turning into a lifestyle similar to the military.

Chapter 7

It wasn't the workout routine that killed us. In fact, it was a pretty easy routine to follow. It was the early mornings that bothered us most. We tried going to bed early, but staying up late was a hard habit to break. After a half hour in the weight lifting room, we showered and were ready for class. Class dragged for the first few hours as we struggled to stay awake, but the rest of the day went by quickly once we started thinking about after school. We were excited for our first day of practice.

Finally, it was here. We put on our practice jerseys for the first time, and really felt like part of the team. We walked onto the practice field with pride as we were part of a strong tradition. Practice started off with a few minutes of exercising. Some of the drills we did were similar to the drills we completed with the coach the previous day. The drills, however, were slightly easier the second time. I thought it might be due to the morning of weight lifting, but I'm pretty sure it was just adrenaline.

After stretching, exercising, and speed drills, we were broken up into small groups. Mike was put into a group of runners. They called those guys running backs, who were instructed by the running backs coach. All they did was hold on to the football and run as hard, and as fast, as they could. My group was made of blockers and tacklers. This group was a little unique because it broken into two separate groups, yet we all had the same coach, the line coach. One group, the offensive linemen, played when our team had the ball. Their goal was to make sure our quarterback didn't get tackled while trying to throw the ball. The other group, the defensive linemen, played when our opponent had the ball. Their goal was to tackle the guy with the ball, usually the running back or quarterback.

There were 12 guys total in our group. A starting offensive line consisted of five players, while a starting defensive line generally consisted of four, for a total of nine starters. That meant that at the very least, I would be one of three backup players; which in turn meant more playing time for me than I expected. The line coach quickly ruined my joy by telling us that some of our guys would be starting on both the offensive and defensive line. I soon understood the importance of being in such good shape. Not only did we have to be strong enough to tackle or block, and fast enough to catch the guy with the ball, but we also had to be able to play long periods of time with very little breaks.

We spent about two hours working on plays that day. The plays were pretty easy for us to remember because our roles pretty much stayed the same for every play. Once the ball was snapped, the offensive linemen stood and blocked the guy in front of them while making room for the running back. The defensive linemen had to run through the offensive linemen in an effort to tackle the guy with the ball. The logistics seemed easy enough, but again, the struggle was keeping up with everyone while only taking limited breaks.

Mike didn't have it as easy as I did. I thought the simple concept was to run every time he got the ball. What I didn't realize was the amount of plays he would have to memorize. There were almost 50 plays involving a running back. Sometimes they ran left, sometimes they ran right, sometimes they ran up the middle, and sometimes they didn't run at all. A major challenge for him was that each play was assigned a numeric code. Rather than the head coach telling each player what they had to do, he would give signals to the quarterback, who would then say something silly to the offense like "34 iso". Due to the intense memorization required to know what each numeric code meant, Mike was forced to divide our designated studying time between doing homework, studying for exams, and memorizing plays.

Chapter 8

The next day started off easier to the one before. We were able to fall asleep early the night before because of the long day, which made us more refreshed when we woke up at dawn. We were able to lift more weight and run a little longer. And after struggling through class, we made it to our second practice. Practice was a little different the second time.

I was taught in practice the previous day how to block and how to tackle. With my large size, blocking was easy. With a little more strength, I felt my blocking could've been the best on the team. As a defender, I didn't get a chance to deliver my first tackle. Instead, we continued working on getting past the offensive line, which was where being a big guy helped. Waiting for the snap was another issue, though. As I mentioned earlier, our job was to simply block or tackle as soon as the ball was snapped. The hard part for me was patiently waiting for the ball to be snapped.

With all the excitement and adrenaline going on, I found it hard to wait patiently. That was clearly my biggest struggle and was addressed promptly. The line coach figured out a very effective way of helping me. Every time I jumped early, our entire group would have to do push-ups. As much as I hated push-ups, I really hated letting down the entire group. Needless to say, it didn't take long for me to break that ugly habit.

Mike had an ugly habit to break of his own. While we were working on our drills, we all stopped suddenly when we heard a loud pop. After looking around, I saw the running backs coach talking to Mike with a football laying at his feet. Mike later told me that as he was running a drill, the running backs coach calmly walked up to him and was able to punch the ball out of his grasp. As fast as he was, Mike struggled to hold onto the ball. He wasn't used to carrying things while running, so he simply wasn't paying attention to the ball. The coach made it very clear that even though he was our fastest player on our team, he was a major liability if he couldn't hold onto the ball. That meant that until he could learn to hold onto the ball better, he wouldn't be able to play during the games.

His bad habit was quickly corrected too. As much as he was worried about letting the team down, his biggest motivation was being able to play in the games. There were four other guys trying out for the starting running back position. With that much competition, he would have to be nearly perfect to stand out. We were already informed that we wouldn't be able to start in the game coming up, so we both made it our goal to stand out and become starters the following week.

Chapter 9

My big moment finally came when we got into our big group on Wednesday. After our first water break, we were told that we would be put in to game situations. Our starting offense would run their normal plays, while our second-string defense would run the plays used by our opponent's defense. Our second-string offense would then run the plays of our opponent's offense, while our first-string defense tried to defend against those new plays. The best part was that we were finally allowed to go full contact. That meant I would get my first chance to hit someone. Even though I would be pretending to be a defender from the other team, the tackle would not be a pretend hit.

When one of the defensive linemen on the second-string team was asked to come out, I was told to go in and take his place. I was positioned at the end of the defensive line, known as a defensive end. Our defensive captain told us that we would be defending a run play. My job was to stand across from the offensive tackle. As soon as the ball was snapped, *and not a moment before*, I would have to get around the tackle and hit the guy with the ball. I must not've been taken very seriously, because they decided to run the play towards my side of the field. The running back must not've taken me seriously either, because after I crashed through the offensive line, the he looked shocked.

There was no one between the two of us. Even though the entire moment took seconds, it felt like minutes. I can still remember every detail. I was well trained in waiting for the ball to snap. Once the ball was exchanged between the center and the quarterback, I wasted no time in introducing myself to the tackle across from me. I was so excited to hit someone that I put both arms out in front of me and pushed with all my body weight. The force was strong enough to knock him down to the ground. But I knew I didn't have time to celebrate; getting through that blocker wasn't the end goal. After jumping over the tackle, the running back was next. I suddenly had tunnel vision and locked my focus on the ball carrier.

He looked straight at me, as if I were a speeding train and he was a damsel tied to the tracks. Within seconds, my body engulfed his as I put my arms around him and kept driving. It was like an out of body experience. I had never been that fast, or that strong, in all my life. I had no idea where it was coming from, but I liked it. All of the sudden, the runner was in the air. I felt like a kid holding onto a stuffed animal. Then, in one big move, we both hit the ground. All three of us hit hard; me, him, and the ball. I wasn't sure if they were cheering for my hit, or the touchdown that was ran in by my defense after the ball was knocked free, but I couldn't wait to do it again.

Chapter 10

My first game would be another day that I would never forget. We were allowed to take game day off from lifting because the coach didn't want any injuries. As part of the team, we were able to wear our game jerseys to school so that we could show them off during class. We wore those aqua blue jerseys with pride. We were part of an elite group that would soon be on display for the entire community to watch.

After school, we had some free time. We all went off as a team to eat before the game. A couple hours before game time, we met in the locker room to get dressed. The locker room was full of excitement as the team was preparing for our first game of the season. Finally, the coach was ready to show us off.

We huddled up around the exit of the locker room. It felt like we were in a movie theatre during a fire alarm and the theatre only had one exit. As we were getting ready to burst out of the locker room, Mike and I took one final look at each other and smiled. We joined the crowd of football players as we made our way on to the field. The stadium wasn't as full as it could've been, but the atmosphere was defiantly electric. I could hear the vender trying to sell programs, I could smell the fresh popped popcorn, and I could see the stadium lights being used for the first time that season.

After going through some quick drills, we went back into the locker room. The coach gave us a locker room speech similar to those seen in inspirational sports movies. After the speech, my game-day nerves were replaced by chills of excitement. Again, we were escorted out of the locker room. That time, however, we stopped just short of the field. Once stopped, I was able to soak in the atmosphere. Suddenly, the stadium was packed. We felt like gladiators walking into the arena, prepared for battle.

The crowd was quiet, and the sun was shining bright behind the press box. In front of us, two rows of cheerleaders created a human tunnel for us. At the end of the tunnel was a large banner facing the home crowd, held up by more cheerleaders. After we heard "and now you're EAST WHITAKER HORNETS" broadcasted over the loud speaker system, we ran through the cheerleader tunnel, towards the home crowd, and crashed through the banner. The crowd erupted.

Once everything calmed back down, it was time for kickoff. That was the first time the two of us had ever seen a live football game in person; until then, we had only seen games on television. For 55 minutes, we were part of the home crowd, watching the game from the sidelines. For the last five minutes, we were part of the team.

We were up by 35 points. Because we had the game in hand, the coach was going to let Mike and I play. Mike went out there first. His job was to catch the ball after their punter kicked it. After catching the ball perfectly, he was gone. No one could touch him. Our guys couldn't even keep up with him to block. The entire crowd stood up and cheered as he crossed the goal line. The band played the fight song. The coach was so excited that he threw his hat on the ground. When Mike came back to the sideline, the coach told him to be ready for next week.

Once the other team got the ball back, it was my turn. I don't remember what the play was, but I remember my job was to tackle the ball carrier. It happened just like it happened in practice: I went through the offensive tackle like a freight train, I got tunnel vision, and I ran to the guy with the ball. Believe it or not, I hit their quarterback harder than I hit my teammate in practice. In fact, I hit him so hard that it took a few minutes for him to get back up. The backup quarterback had to come in and play the rest of the game for him.

I heard the crowd cheering for me. I felt the high fives from my proud teammates. I just didn't know what to do next. In practice, after my hit, my team got the ball back. That time, however, the other team still had the ball and we were still on defense. Then I heard our defensive leader yelling for me to join the huddle. We were preparing for a running play. I went back to the line and again exploded once the ball was snapped. That time, the running back ran away from me, so I had to let one of my teammates tackle him. I liked it better when I got to tackle someone; I wanted more plays like that.

Chapter 11

We finally had a chance to enjoy a weekend. Of course, there had always been weekends before, but we never had a chance to truly appreciate them for what they were. After four days of practices, three days of working out, and one game, we had two days off to ourselves where we could relax - and relax we did. We slept until noon and didn't do much after that. Our days of partying all weekend seemed to be on hold during the season.

After the restful weekend, it was back to the weekly routine. In our small group sessions, we were able to talk about specific issues from the previous game. The line coach spent the entire weekend reviewing game footage and analyzed what we could do to improve. We spent the whole day working on not moving until the ball was snapped. Although that seemed like my biggest problem during practice the previous week, it apparently was a common problem for the rest of the guys during the game.

At the end of practice, the line coach got us together and told us who would be starting in the second game of the season. The starting line changed a little bit, but the biggest change for me was the pecking order of backup players. My name was at the top of the list, which meant that as soon as one of the starters needed a break, I would get my chance to play. With three guys playing both offense and defense, I knew I wouldn't be on the sideline for very long. With that news, I was motivated to push myself even harder that week. I was going to prove to the coaches that they had made the right decision.

Mike was just as motivated as I was. His group got together during practice as well to discuss their starters. After his impressive punt return last week, he earned a spot as the starting punt and kick returner. He was also selected to be the number one backup running back. Just like with me, if the starting running back needed a break, or wasn't doing well, Mike would be the first one out to relieve him.

As second teamers, we were given the opportunity to play an entire scrimmage against the first teamers on Wednesday. In the previous week, we were only allowed to play a few plays. This week, however, we were able to play a majority of the time, while showing off our progress. We knew that even though the coaches would be paying the most attention to the starters, they would know right away if one of us screwed up.

At the end of Thursday's practice, the head coach reminded the team that the next day would be an away game. Once everyone was dismissed, the he asked Mike and I to stay and talk with him. He began by telling us how impressed he was with our performance over the last few days. It was clear to him that we were dedicated, motivated, and using our time wisely in the gym. He was also impressed with our performance during the game. He didn't know what to expect from us after a short week of practice for two kids who have never played football before, especially after only a week of practice. He defiantly wasn't expecting a quarterback sack and a punt return for a touchdown.

His last point, he emphasized, was more important than our improvement in play, or our improvement in the gym. What he was the most impressed about was the improvement in our classes. Although they hadn't received any of our grades yet, the teachers made it clear to the coach that we were making the most of our studying time, and for once, we went the first two weeks of the school year without missing a single class. The coach then told us that no matter how good we were on the football field, we were only as good as our grades.

Chapter 12

Just like the first week, we skipped working out on game day. And again, we were able to parade around school in our game jerseys at school. We were defiantly excited for our second game, and a chance to get more playing time, but we were even more excited to go on a road trip with the rest of the team. It was going to be our chance to feel like professional football players.

After school, the team met in the locker room. Most of the guys were goofing around and having a good time. It was clear that Mike and I weren't the only excited ones. Once we were all dressed and had our gear ready, the head coach came into the locker room. He told us how important this game was. He reminded us that we were men representing our school. We would be going to a new city and showing them what an East Whitaker Hornet really was. Because of the responsibility, we were held to a higher standard. At that point, the locker room got really serious, and all smiles were gone. We realized that fun time was over. We had a job to do.

Once everyone was on the bus, we were all quiet. Most players had headphones on, while others simply stared out the window, but all of us were thinking the same thing; what we would have to do to come home winners. The only noise heard on that bus was the sound of players eating their pre-game meal and the coaches discussing game plans.

After the short 20 minute ride, the busses stopped outside of the stadium. We were escorted to the visiting team locker room, which was painted pink. We quickly got dressed and went onto the field to do some last minute drills and stretching. The stadium wasn't very full, but I knew that would change once it got closer to game time. As excited as Mike and I were, it felt different compared to the previous game. Last week, we were two kids who made the football team and would only play if the score got out of hand. This week, we were part of the team, and we had a real chance of making a difference in the game.

After the coach's pre-game speech in the locker room, we went back out to the field. I suddenly felt an eerie feeling. It felt like we didn't belong there. Instead of cheers upon our arrival into the packed stadium, we heard boos. There wasn't a cheerleader tunnel, or a large banner to run through. We went directly to the sideline. It was as if we were wasting the fans' time just by being there. Once the other team came out of the locker room, they made it very clear that they were the home team and *we* would have to steal the victory from *them*.

Chapter 13

It didn't take long for Mike to get his first chance of playing. Our defense held their offense to only three plays before they had to give the ball back to us. I think the other team watched our previous game because they were ready for Mike. During his first game, no one knew what he was capable of, so as soon as Mike got the ball, he simply ran straight ahead and was never touched. Now, our opponent knew what he was capable of, and knew they would have to stop him right away. Mike didn't make it far, but at least he made positive yardage. He got another chance to play when our starting running back lost yardage on a play. Once our quarterback handed Mike the ball, he was gone. Just like that, he scored his second touchdown.

Although he didn't score a touchdown every time he touched the ball, Mike made the most of his opportunities whenever he got called back in. I didn't get my chance to play until halfway through the 2nd quarter. One of our offensive linemen needed a break, so I came in for him. After a few plays of not letting anyone get by me, the starter was ready to come back in.

Going into the locker room at halftime, we were up by 20. The coach wanted us to keep playing our game without making any changes. Even though we had a big lead, he said a lot could happen in 24 minutes. That meant we were still stuck on the sidelines. However, Mike would still get a few chances to improve his punt returning ability.

We remained backups until the 4th quarter. We were up by 24 points, so the coach wanted to bench the starters to protect them from injury. I became the starting defensive end, while Mike took over at running back. He continued to add yards to his already impressive performance, as well as another touchdown. I was able to add a tackle behind the line of scrimmage and, while on offense, I didn't let anyone get by me.

At the end of four quarters, we were able to silence the crowd. We took their energy and became the loud ones. We huddled up on the middle of their field like we owned it, and no one was going to challenge us. We sang our school fight song, then ran onto the bus and headed home.

On the way back from the game, the atmosphere was just the opposite of what it was on the way to the game. Everyone was yelling and cheering, while the coaches were bragging about successful plays. Mike and I were even congratulated by some of our teammates.

When we got back to the school, a large group of parents were waiting for us. As we got off the bus, the large crowd broke into the school's fight song. Once we were all off the bus, we joined in with them. Then, after singing, the weirdest thing happened. While Mike and I were talking to our parents about the game, a couple of teammates approached us. Out of nowhere, they invited us to the post-game party. If there was ever a time when we questioned if we were actually part of the team, that invitation squashed all doubt.

Chapter 14

Before long, it was obvious why we were invited to that party; they wanted to celebrate with Mike. Although I had a few good plays myself, the guys kept telling Mike that he would probably be a starter soon. That prediction came true a few days later at practice. Just like the previous week, we were given our game assignments in our small groups. I would continue to be the first backup, but Mike got promoted to starting running back, as well as special team's returner.

Later in the week, our team was being prepped by the head coach for the upcoming game. Although most of the guys already knew what the coach was saying, it was news to Mike and I. Apparently, the first two games we played were non-conference games. They were known as "tune-up games" and wins or loses didn't count towards our conference record. Those results would, however, count towards our overall season record, which would determine if we would be eligible to play in the state tournament. Our conference record, meanwhile, would determine which team in our conference had the best record at the end of the season, with a trophy going to that team. It was a trophy that our school had only won a handful of times. Of course the goal that year was to win the trophy, but the bigger goal was to go undefeated the entire season. East Whitaker had only been able to do that once during the regular season, but couldn't do it during the post-season.

The coach went on to explain that the game Friday would not only be our first conference game of the season, but could be our third victory in a row. That gave us a new motivation. Now those games meant even more. We weren't just trying to win games, we were trying to accomplish something that had never been done before.

Our first conference game in the Becker County Conference would be a game that would either put us on the map in the conference, or would let other teams know that we were all talk. Even though we had already achieved two victories, we were now playing against some tougher competition. I think that's what made Mike the most nervous.

Mike would be the starting running back for our team during the first conference game of the season. If the coaches made a bad decision in promoting him, we risked losing the game, as well as our perfect season. If he did well, he would have to play at that superstar level all season. Mike felt like he was carrying the season in his hands. Sure, he had good games the first two weeks, but as the coach pointed out, those were teams that couldn't compete with us. Mike would he have to dominate the teams in our conference the way he did in our "tune-up games".

Chapter 15

Shockingly, that game ended up being Mike's best game. He had 3 touchdowns, nearly 200 rushing yards, and figured out how to run back a punt return without just going in a straight line. That was one of my best games, too. As an offensive lineman, no one got past me. As a defensive lineman, I had 2 tackles and 1 sack.

After that victory, those stats would stay pretty constant for the next few weeks. Even though I was putting up impressive numbers, I was still just a backup. I was getting stronger, but I still wasn't as strong as the other guys on the defensive line. At one point, I asked the coach why I was still on the sideline, even though I was seeing so much success on the field. He told me that as a backup, opponents were unfamiliar with my playing style. They were used to the abilities of the starter, so when I relieved the starter, they didn't have enough time to figure me out. If, however, I became a starter, teams would be able to stop me once they spent some time scouting me. The coach reassured me that if I continued to get stronger, eventually no team would be able to stop me, no matter how much they studied me.

I was slightly confused by his logic, but it sunk in when I watched Mike on the field. Once he became a starter, opponents knew his moves and could create defensive plays to try and stop him. But because of his speed and quick turns, those plays were irrelevant because they still couldn't catch him. I knew I would soon be in his shoes as long as I kept working hard in the gym and at practice. Rather than being discouraged by what the coach told me, I used it as motivation. In fact, throughout the weeks, my workouts became even more intense.

After winning our next four games in a row, Mike was a star. With 13 touchdowns, he was on track to break the school's record for most touchdowns in a season. Fans would cheer every time he got the ball, and students would go out of their way to get his attention at school. He didn't let it go to his head, though. Even though I remained a backup for the rest of the regular season, he never put himself above me.

As the season went on, our grades continued to improve. Not only did we continue to work out in the early mornings, we also continued to study late at night. Mike maintained a C average, while I was getting Bs. Our grades were going up, we were getting faster, we were getting stronger, and our popularity was growing. Even though I wasn't a starter, I was still earning a reputation as one of the team's hardest hitters. I even had the most tackles for loss on our team.

In the six weeks of conference play, the team's excitement and intensity remained consistent. As we continued to win, we were getting closer to that perfect record. We all shared the same goal of maintaining that perfect record, and we were committed to work together as a team to achieve it. Whatever we were doing was clearly working, so there was no need to mess with our finely tuned machine. All of that changed, however, during the last week of the regular season.

Chapter 16

It was rivalry week. That game meant more than just a win. That game would be a reflection of the type of season we had. If we lost that game, we had a bad season. If we won that game, we had a great season. That game would give us an undefeated season. An undefeated season would rank us high in the state playoffs. It would also be our last home game. That meant the seniors would be playing their last regular season game at East Whitaker High School. Clearly, that group of seniors didn't want to go out as losers. Most importantly, that game was against our biggest rival, the West Whitaker Wolves. Beating West Whitaker would give us bragging rights, while stopping *their* undefeated season. There was no way we were going to let them ruin our season.

Even Monday's practice started off differently. In our positional groups, our coaches were more intense than usual. Their voices were louder than normal, and there was no horsing around. Their attitudes made the rest of the team act seriously because nobody wanted to upset those coaches. That seriousness led to harder hits in practice, and the entire team seemed to all be on the same page.

Up until that game, we were on a winning streak. We expected to win games because that's just what we did. We were excited about games, but we were lacking the intensity. The West Whitaker week had a different feel, though. It felt as if it was a playoff game and the result of the game would make, or brake, our season. For that, we had to give it our all at practice and leave nothing behind. We had to hit as hard as we could, we had to run as fast as we could, and we had to move as soon as the ball was snapped... every time. And anytime we didn't do any of something correctly, it was 20 push-ups.

Our Wednesday scrimmage even felt like a real game. The coaches would get irate if any of the starters messed up and would make them correct themselves three times over just to make sure they did it correctly. Even the backup team was playing intense and would also be corrected on any mistakes. It was the most intense week of practice ever. There was no way we were going to lose to those West Whitaker Weenies.

Thursday was more of a celebratory practice. The coach reminded the seniors that the following day would be their last home game. He wanted us to celebrate our last regular season practice. Although we would have to practice during the playoffs, he wanted to celebrate us surviving the 11 grueling weeks of practice that led us to the playoffs. Finally, we were taking time to celebrate because we wouldn't have another chance to celebrate until the playoffs were over. Once we beat West Whitaker, it was time to start the post-season. Every waking moment would be dedicated to winning games, and we wouldn't have time to celebrate victories.

Even at school, the atmosphere was intense. The students knew how important that game was. They went out of their way that week to show off their school spirit. Every student wore aqua blue and dark purple, our team colors. We were dismissed from school at the end of every day that week with the fight song playing on the P.A. system. The best display of school spirit, though, was the prep rally.

School was put on hold for an hour, while the entire student body met in the gym. Just like on the field, we came crashing through the gym doors once we were announced, and were greeted by a full audience of cheers. When we stood in the middle of the basketball court, we saw cheerleaders with their faces painted, students with their aqua blue and dark purple clothing, signs, banners, and even air horns. We suddenly realized that we weren't just playing the game for us, we were playing for the entire school.

Chapter 17

Before every home game, the locker room carried a relaxed attitude. However, before the West Whitaker game, the locker room was silent. We looked like men on a mission. The entire team knew what was at stake. We would have to give all our time, energy, and attention to that game. As we made it to the field for our pre-game stretches, we walked in unison. For the first time that season, we walked out to a sold-out stadium an hour before the game even started.

Back in the locker room, the coach gave another great speech. He reminded us how important the game was, not just to the team, but to the seniors as well. He made us realize how great it would feel to achieve an undefeated season at home against West Whitaker, while the entire town watched. Then, it was game time.

Although the team remained quiet, it still wasn't silent in the locker room. We could hear music. As we opened the locker room door, the music got louder. We could see the high school marching band on the field. The band usually played before the game, and at halftime, but they were never on the field when we left the locker room.

All of the sudden, the music stopped. The only noise was coming from one single drum, making a simple beat that seemed to keep the band in step as they started to march into a formation. In less than a minute, the band created a human tunnel; similar to the cheerleader tunnel, but ten times bigger. As they began to play the fight song, the fans in the bleachers stood up, sang along, and clapped to the beat. Then, like a herd of cattle, our team ran through the tunnel.

As I was running through the tunnel, I had a momentary flashback to the day in the auditorium when we turned down the band because we were too cool for them. As a football player, you knew about the band. You knew they played while the team was in the locker room, but they were never considered part of the football program. However, at that moment, that big group of band nerds, the group that we walked away from, had suddenly become part of our team. The band even stayed on the sidelines during the game. They played music to pep up the crowd, and would play the fight song every time we scored.

Halfway through the 2nd quarter, the score was tied. With the anxiety at an all-time high, I heard someone behind me yelling to the crowd for an "H". Without wasting any time, the crowd fulfilled his order. Next, he asked for an "O". And again, the crowd didn't skip a beat. As I turned around to see what was going on, I saw an elderly man dressed from head to toe in dark purple and aqua blue standing up with his hands on either side of his mouth screaming loudly for an "R". He continued until the crowd spelled H-O-R-N-E-T-S. Standing next to him was a younger man, also dressed head to toe in our school colors, banging on a cowbell. The atmosphere was charged as the crowd became louder than the cheerleaders.

We went into the locker room at halftime with the game still tied. The coach told us that we were doing everything right, and there was no need to get discouraged. We practiced hard, and that hard work would pay off as the game went on. He told us the reason behind the intensity of the practices leading up to that game wasn't just to work on plays for the game, we were also working on enduring the speed and tempo of a high-paced game. It was that increased endurance achieved through practice that would help us win the game.

The game remained tied until the last few minutes of the 4th quarter. Mike returned a punt and put us 40 yards away from the end zone. After three unsuccessful deep throws by our quarterback, we had one chance left to score before sending the game into overtime. We were already exhausted from battle, so overtime would feel like a second game to us. We were more than willing to give all that we had left to end the game there. Unfortunately, we were too far out for our kicker to attempt a field goal, so we had to come up with one play that would get us those 40 yards. During the time out, I was asked to join the offensive huddle. I figured I would be used on the offensive line, so I was in complete shock when the coach told the team that I would be getting the ball. He told me that their defense would never see it coming, my size would be hard to take down, and my speed had increased to the point where I could be trusted with the ball.

From the huddle, I went to stand on the offensive line next to the tackle. Once the ball was snapped, I ran over to the quarterback, who then handed me the ball. By the time their defense realized I had the ball, I was already 10 yards ahead of the line of scrimmage. At that point, it was a foot race to the goal line between me and the entire Wolf defense. Although my speed had increased, I still wasn't as fast as most of their defenders. With that 10-yard head start, I was able to keep a distance until the 7-yard line. By then, I had so much momentum, nothing was going to take me down. Suddenly, with the weight of three defenders on my back, I struggled to move as the weight was too much to take. I could feel my teammates pushing me into the end zone, but it wasn't enough as my legs gave

out. I fell down hard, like a tall tree cut down in the woods.
Then... silence.

Did I blow it? Did I let down the team, the coaches,
the town? After what felt like minutes of silence, I finally
had my answer. There was that familiar fight song I knew
so well, the eruption of the crowd, the entire team tackling
me in the end zone. Mike might have been our best player,
braking the school record that night for both the most
rushing yards and the most touchdowns in a season, but I
won the game. I made us perfect.

Chapter 18

Just like the coach said, there wasn't any time to celebrate. Monday began another week of practice. And just like last weeks practice, it was intense. The coach said the reason why West Whitaker was able to hang with us for so long was that our defense got tired. For the playoffs, the coach was going to substitute his defensive players more often. That meant that I would get more game time. I knew I wouldn't get another season-winning touchdown, but at least I could have some playoff-winning sacks.

Our first game in the playoffs was a cake walk. Because we had a perfect record, we were paired against a team who had won only half of their games. By halftime, we were up by 5 touchdowns, 3 of those belonging to Mike. Meanwhile, I had 3 tackles for loss. In the 2nd half, his playing time was over, but mine was just beginning. My stats got even better. Towards the end of the game, I hit their quarterback so hard that he lost the ball. Because of my conditioning, I was able to quickly get up after the hit, rather than stay on the ground. Once I got up, I saw the ball still laying there so I picked it up. I quickly realized that the play hadn't stopped yet because I soon had a swarm of defenders coming at me. I had nothing else to do but to run. Just like that, I scored my second touchdown in two weeks. We were now going to the second round of playoffs without being scored on.

Our second round game wasn't quite a blowout. Mike had multiple touchdowns, but our defense couldn't stop the other team from scoring. I didn't have any touchdowns, or sacks, but I did have one tackle for loss, which contributed to a second round 21-point victory.

The following week, we were playing for the regional finals. We had to play against one of the toughest teams in the state. They were a team that made it to the state semi-finals six out of the last seven years. They knew what Mike was capable of, and clearly spent all week planning against him. They held him to under 100 yards with no touchdowns. What they didn't plan for was our passing game. As great a player as Mike was, we still had an all-conference quarterback who could throw a really deep ball, and two senior receivers who could catch that ball. After fooling them by faking the run and instead scoring three deep touchdowns in a row, we took a 7-point lead into the 4th quarter. From there, our defense did the rest. The coach's idea of subbing us out continually paid off, as our fresh defensive players wore them down and stopped them from gaining any yardage the entire 4th quarter.

For the first time in school history, we were in the state semi-finals. It would be our last step on our way to the state finals. We would have to play against the defending champion. We practiced that week the same way we had all playoffs, and we played that game like we had played every game that season, but for whatever reason, they weren't ready for us. For the entire 1st half, we scored every time we got the ball. Two of those scores came from Mike's punt returns.

In the 2nd half, we had such a commanding lead that the coach felt comfortable benching our starters for the rest of the game. The sideline was still all business, though, and there weren't any early celebrations. Even though we had the game in hand, we didn't want to lose it. Going into the last play of the game, I had 1 sack. After ending the game with another sack, it was official; we were on our way into the state finals.

Chapter 19

The week leading up to the championship game was similar to the West Whitaker rivalry week. It was very intense, the coaches were very serious, and the players were very quiet. Every day, the student body showed a different way to display their school spirit. We continued our normal practice routine, and stuck with the same game plan that got us to the state finals. Even the coach's speech on Thursday was similar. He wanted us to know how proud we should be, and how proud he was of us. We had made it pretty far, but our journey wasn't done yet. At that moment, we really did feel proud. We had an undefeated season, we beat West Whitaker at home, and we stormed our way through the playoffs. Adding a state championship to the season would make it the best season ever; a season Mike and I would be proud to help build.

The following day, another prep rally was held in the gym. It served as a good reminder of who we were representing, but it wasn't as exciting as the West Whitaker prep rally because it wasn't a surprise. What we weren't expecting was the prep rally held the following day.

We were told to meet at the high school early Saturday morning to board the buses heading to Lansing. We were going to play our game in the same stadium where Michigan's professional football team, the Michigan Knights, played. We would be on live television, watched by fans, coaches, players, and even scouts from all over the state. But as we left the locker rooms to board the buses, we were speechless. In front of us were four luxury buses. They were the buses with televisions on the ceiling, and bathrooms that really worked. Surrounding those buses were nearly 3,000 students, parents, and neighbors with signs, banners, and even the cowbell. We were even more surprised when we saw numerous people from West Whitaker show up to support us. At the West Whitaker rally, we realized that we were playing for the pride of the 2,000 students at East Whitaker High. Five weeks later, we realized that we would be fighting for the 100,000 residents of Becker County.

Chapter 20

It was hard not to show any emotion on the way to the game. There was so much going on in my head. Just a few months ago, Mike and I were at the Becker County Jail; a fast kid and his fat friend. A short time later, we morphed into an athletic tackler and his record-breaking friend on their way to the state finals. I thought about the opportunity of playing where the Michigan Knights played. Prior to the season, I was never able to witness a football game in person. An hour later, not only would I be able to see the famous stadium, I would be on the field and on the big screen. Of course, I also thought about the buses. I felt like a celebrity on the bus.

After an hour on the road, we were at the stadium. We felt like professional football players when we got off the bus. Within minutes, we were dressing where the Michigan Knights dressed. Even our locker room pep talk had a different feel. We were getting a speech from our coach about leaving it all on the field in the same locker room where legendary coaches gave their great speeches to professional football players.

Finally, it was time. We walked out of the tunnel and onto the field. It was breath taking. It was the biggest indoor facility I had ever seen. The place could've held a million people. Looking in the stands, I saw a lot of aqua blue and dark purple; fans that made the voyage to support us. Directly across the field from them was a mass of blue and yellow. Apparently, the other team had a big following as well. We had to remember that they made the same journey we did, and we were the only two football teams still playing in the state of Michigan.

It didn't take long to realize how our opponents made it to the playoffs. It was intimidating enough when they came onto the field. Those guys looked like a college football team as they came out of the locker room. They were strong, they were fast, and they never got tired.

Much like in the regional final game, they planned against Mike. After shutting him down numerous times, we discovered that they also planned against our passing. We went the entire game without a score. Our defense stayed strong, but without being able to put points up, it didn't take much to outscore us. After 48 depressing minutes, we finally got a chance to experience loss.

And what an emotional loss it was. Our big, tough guys were crying. Our coaches were quiet. There was no fight song at the end of the game. It hit us hard. Our perfect season came to a halt one game too soon. We let down our coaches, our fans, and our town. The locker room was silent. No one wanted to say anything, and even if they did, no one wanted to listen. We walked towards the buses with our heads down. We were ready for that long, quiet ride, so that we could go home and shut off the world. We didn't quite make it to the buses before the coach stopped us.

In the tunnel leading to the buses, the head coach had us huddle around him for one last team huddle. The coach said he was disappointed in us, but not because of the loss. We won every game in the regular season. We shattered multiple school records. We had numerous players with a future in college football. We destroyed the path to the state finals. Our only loss came at the end of the season, where we were only one of two teams that made it to the state final to play on live television where the Michigan Knights played professional football. We had absolutely no right to be walking out of that stadium with our heads down.

The coach then reminded us that after the West Whitaker game, he told us we would not be able to celebrate until the playoffs were over. After five long weeks, it was finally time to celebrate. We had a lot to celebrate, and no reason to feel ashamed. We even had a new goal for the following year: win the state championship. Within a few minutes, the buses were loud again and never quieted down. There were a lot of parties that weekend; we were heroes.

Chapter 21

Back at school, we were treated as if we had won the game. Students wouldn't stop talking about the season we had, and how excited they were for the following year. They were even talking about starting a student section so that the students could cheer as a large group, and would even come up with their own cheers.

After class, we were lost. We didn't know what to do. For the last few months, we would go right to practice after school. Once the playoffs were over, though, the season was over. Mike and I had just successfully fulfilled our sentence from the judge and were no longer required to participate in an after-school program. When we were initially sentenced by the judge to participate in something after-school, we were begging for jail. But now that the after-school program was over, we felt a big void in our lives. It didn't feel right.

Shortly after the football season ended, Mike and I talked about the previous season. We came to the conclusion that it was the best few months of our lives. We were really proud of how drastic our lives had changed, and how much fun we had playing football. We then decided that we were willing to do whatever it took to play football together for the rest of our lives. Our goal was to play together on the same professional football team. We eventually took up part-time jobs in the springtime so that we could pay for college. We spent long days working out, and doing our homework, so that we could maintain our strength, speed, and grades. We attempted to work out five days a week, but there were a few days when Mike couldn't make it. He was too busy traveling the country.

Mike had such a good year the previous season that many major college football teams were competing to get him to play for them. These schools were all willing give him a full-ride scholarship. Typically, those schools would fly him to their campus for free, allowing him to check out their program. They would give him a tour of their complexes, would feed him gourmet meals, and would give him behind-the-scenes tours of their athletic facilities. Finally, they would ask Mike to play for them. They would all make him feel like royalty in an effort to win him over. One of them even went so far as to announce his name over the loudspeaker, and display his picture on the big screen while he was touring their football field. Another had the school mascot and a few cheerleaders waiting for his arrival at the airport.

Mike's answer was always the same, though. None of those schools would take the both of us as a package, so he didn't want to make any decisions until I received my offers. We both agreed that we were willing to go out of our way to continue playing together, even if it meant making sacrifices. Unfortunately, I didn't get any offers between the time our first season was over and our second season had begun. All I could do was continue lifting weights and try to make myself a better player for our senior year. We were hoping that after another season, we would both get full offers from the same school. In the meantime, we continued to work our part-time jobs, while working on our grades, just in case my athleticism couldn't get me into college.

Chapter 22

The summer had a different feel to it. The previous summer, we were enjoying our nights. When we weren't causing trouble, we were sleeping late, partying, and doing things that still embarrass me. The following summer, we continued our workouts so that I too could be noticed by college recruiters. We made it our goal for the upcoming year to have it be *my* year so we could be recruited together by the same school. I was willing to make sacrifices, and Mike was more than willing to help me.

My first chance to improve came in the middle of summer. Every summer, the line coach would put on a linemen camp. The camp was a one week session dedicated to both offensive, and defensive, linemen. The practice sessions were four hours long, with a water break when the sun got too hot. During the days, we would do drills to keep in shape, watch videos of last season so we could critique ourselves, and spend time together to create a stronger bond and better communication.

All of the hours that Mike and I spent in the gym made the workouts easier for me. I was the only lineman who could do all of the push-ups, all of the sit-ups, and I was usually one of the first to finish our running. What the weight room didn't prepare me for was the heat. Summers weren't outrageously hot in Michigan, but they sure were humid. The typical weather that week was 90°, with 85% humidity and a cloud here or there to give us eight seconds of shade every 30 minutes. The humidity made it feel like 115°. Just being in that weather for four hours is bad, but running, doing push-ups, and doing sit-ups in that weather was torturous. Luckily, we didn't have to wear pads.

The linemen camp wasn't set up for competition, but I couldn't stop myself from trying to figure out who I would have to compete with if I wanted to become a starter. On the first day of camp, it was obvious who my competition was. Chris Stimson was a sophomore who was so good that he was allowed to bypass the junior varsity team. He was stronger, faster, and had better timing than me. I knew for sure that if I didn't get better, he would take my starting spot.

I spent the entire week at linemen camp pushing myself to do better than him. By the end of those long days, I felt like I was going to pass out. Meanwhile, Chris never seemed phased. He was like a machine. The only chance I had against him was the fact that we never had an opportunity to hit. Even though he was stronger, I still had the chance of delivering a better hit than he could.

Chapter 23

A few weeks later, my plan seemed to backfire. The summer linemen camp was created just for linemen and only involved the line coach. Two-a-day practices were another beast. After the first day, we realized why the other players resented Mike and I the previous year for missing these workouts. Two-a-days included the whole team, involved the entire coaching staff, and lasted two weeks. The workouts were more intense than lineman camp, and lasted the entire day. I felt I could at least use this as an opportunity to impress the head coach and show him that I really could hit the hardest. Unfortunately, that would have to wait too because, just like the linemen camp, there was no hitting allowed.

Two-a-days involved a lot of working out. It also gave the team a chance to work on new strategy. Our strategy was simple. We had one mission: Win the state championship. We would have to do whatever it took to get there. We almost made it the previous year, so the coaches didn't want to change much. They knew that Mike would be the focal point for the team, so they tried to build the team around him. They wanted the offensive line to be stronger, and give him more room to run. They wanted our quarterback to start running with the ball, so we could put in some trick plays. They wanted the receivers to improve so we didn't have to run all the time. Ok, so maybe there were some needed changes, but the strategy for the linemen stayed the same. When on offense, don't let anyone get by; when on defense, tackle the guy with the ball.

Just like last year's regular season practice, the linemen didn't spend too much time working on plays during the two-a-days. We, instead, used those two weeks to stay in shape. That meant we did even more push-ups, sit-ups, and running than we did during linemen camp. During linemen camp, Chris impressed the line coach with his speed, strength, and timing. During the two-a-days, he got a chance to impress the entire coaching staff, and made it even more obvious that the coaches would be foolish if they didn't start him over me. I knew if I couldn't start, I wouldn't be recruited by a major college football team.

While Mike was set to have an even better season than the previous year, he was still aware of my frusteration. He reminded me that I would get my chance once we were allowed to hit. He also pointed out how obvious my progression had been from the previous season. When I first began, I could hardly do one push-up. This year, I was keeping up with the team and not slowing down at all. Mike was even impressed with how well I was handling the heat. He wasn't there for linemen camp, so he didn't get a chance to enjoy that humid Michigan weather.

Chapter 24

Finally, the summer of torture was over. It was time to get into season mode. Our season practices started two weeks before the season officially began. That meant the coaches had two weeks to decide on their starters before we played our first game. Those two weeks were my only opportunity to prove to the coaches that I deserved to be a starter. Once those two weeks were up, the line coach would announce the starters on Monday, and we would spend that week getting ready for the game. Again, to be recruited I knew I would have to start *every* game that season. There was nothing in the world that could've motivated me more. I was in the best shape of my life, I had just finished a successful linemen camp, I had just finished a successful two weeks of two-a-day practices and suddenly, the stage was mine. If I was off on the snaps, behind in the running, or if I let the defender get by me even once, my chances at starting would be over. I used that motivation as a weapon, and didn't waste a minute trying to show the coaches what I could provide the team as a starter.

My time to hit came three days into practice. The head coach got us together to run some plays as a team. He wanted to show us a new play, and wanted to make sure we all understood it. After spending so much time trying to impress the line coach, it was time to impress the head coach. It was a play designed for Mike. I was asked to play on the right side of the line. I couldn't have been more proud at that moment because, in front of the whole team, the coach let me be part of the very first play that season. My proud moment quickly vanished when I looked over and saw Chris on the opposite side of the offensive line. We ran the same play 10 times. In those 10 times, neither of us let the defender through. He and I were equals and my time to impress was running out.

I got another chance to stand out when I was asked to play defense. I was excited because I would finally get a chance to hit someone, and hitting was what I did best. With all the momentum and pressure on my side, I knew I delivered my best hit based on the way the team reacted. Not only was I the one to tackle the running back, but Chris couldn't even get past the offensive lineman. Mike was watching the whole thing and told me that Chris was fast and quick, but couldn't figure out the technique of getting past the lineman. He guessed that his lack of experience was probably a factor.

After two weeks of great hits and heavy competition, Monday finally came. Announcement day was finally here. I was very excited, and yet very nervous. This decision would be my one and only shot at furthering my career as a football player. That moment would tell if Mike and I would continue to play together after high school, or go off on our separate ways. Finally, the list. The coach read off the names of the five offensive starters; mine wasn't one of them...Chris' was. In my mind my career was over, and our dream had been cancelled. That young punk wasn't even part of our team last year, yet he was given the right to take *my* starting spot. The line coach continued talking, but I was so upset that I tuned him out. I was actually fighting tears.

Suddenly I was being congratulated by some of my friends. They said they knew how hard I had been working, and knew I deserved what I got. I started to take it personal until I finally snapped out of it. I had forgotten that we also had four *defensive* starters, which gave me four additional chances to start. Three of those spots went to starting offensive linemen, the fourth went to me. I was so obsessed with beating my competitor that I forgot we were all fighting for more than one starting role. I finally had my chance to start. More importantly, I would finally have a chance to show my new talents to major college football scouts.

Chapter 25

Just when I thought it couldn't get any better, Mike and I were called into the coach's office. On the first Monday of the regular season, Mike and I had a private conversation with the coach for the second year in a row. The previous year, we had been accepted onto the team as long as we kept our grades in line. At that time, we were out of shape kids ordered by the court to find a second chance to better ourselves and hopefully stay out of jail. Exactly one year later, Mike was the running back that carried our team to the state finals. I was in the best shape of my life and was declared one of the two best linemen on the East Whitaker varsity football team. Just a few moments ago, we were both named starters; a few minutes later, we were both declared team captains!

The coach made it clear that captains were the leaders of the team. We would be the ones that would represent the team, and would have to display the personality of leaders. Although we didn't have much experience in leadership, our dedication and commitment to the team was inspiring the rest of the team to keep up at our level. Playing for the team took more than skill and ability; it took drive and hard work. Because of our drive and hard work last season, we were trusted to lead the team.

Being a captain came with a lot of reward and recognition, but it also came with a lot of responsibility. Our first responsibility was to lead the team in stretches and warm ups during practices. We also had to speak to the team in smaller groups to motivate them. Mike would talk to the offense, being the offensive captain, and I would talk to the defense. We had to make sure that the team played at our level of determination and continued to increase their speed and strength at practice. It was our job to make them look good, and it was their job not to make us look bad.

On game day, the job became fun. It was up to us to lead the team out of the locker room. Behind us stood nearly 60 players, in front of us was a sold out crowd. As we exited the locker room, I noticed two sections of bleachers on our side of the field filled with students, all wearing aqua and dark purple, with a large sign that read "EAST WHITAKER HORNET'S NEST".

Once we were out of the locker room, we marched in unison towards the cheerleader tunnel. When our team was introduced, it was our responsibility to lead the pack crashing through the cheerleaders' banner at the end of the tunnel. For only a second, I flashed on being the last ones through the tunnel the previous season. After Mike and I were called out to the middle of the field for the traditional coin toss, it was back to the sidelines to get the team ready for an exciting 48 minutes of play.

The first game of the season was turning into a blowout. Instead of getting a chance to relieve the starters halfway through the 3rd quarter, we were the ones being relieved. As we ran off the field, we knew we were going to do awesome that season. Not only were we up by 48 points; we had just produced the best statistical game of both our careers. He carried the ball 6 times across the goal line and ran for over 200 yards. I tackled the running back 4 times behind the line of scrimmage and took out the quarterback twice. I also caused a fumble that led to another touchdown. We knew that if we continued to play like that, we would be playing together for the rest of our lives.

Chapter 26

After a weekend of celebrating an awesome Friday night game, it was time to get back to business. The coaches were very pleased with us as a team, but reminded us that we still had eight games to go. The team that we had just beaten didn't have the skill level remotely comparable to the team we would be playing in the second week. We couldn't look past the upcoming game. We would have to look at that game, and every game that season, as a playoff game if we wanted to be champions.

We all ran fast, hit hard, and exploded off the line at practice that week. In our small groups, I kept watching my former competitor, Chris. He was young and didn't have much athletic skill, but was big and strong and used that to his advantage. As an offensive lineman, it took strength to keep the defender out of our backfield. Because of that, he was our best offensive lineman. On the defensive line, however, it took skill and talent to find a way to elude the offender, which made him one of our worst defensive linemen. As a competitor, I would've laughed at him, but as a captain, I knew it was up to me to help him.

After practice, I took Stimpson to the side. I remembered how embarrassed I was when the coach pointed out my flaws in front of the whole team the previous season, so I wanted to help him privately. I began by explaining how competitive he forced me to be during the off-season. As teammates, though, I was happy to be on his side. I told him it was too bad that he could only contribute on the offensive side because of his defensive limitations. I then told him how powerful we would be if he could be on the defensive line with me. At that point, he admitted that he needed help. I wasn't sure how to tell him he was struggling, so I was relieved when he did it for me.

After working with him for nearly an hour, our hard work would pay off the following day during practice. Stimpson still wasn't the best defensive lineman, but he didn't seem to struggle as much. I knew with a little bit of practice, he could be used as a defensive substitute when our guys got tired. Once, when we were practicing with the second team defense, he was put in as a defensive lineman. While watching him get past the offender, I felt like I was watching myself from the previous season. He had the same reaction; he was shocked that he had achieved the small victory and didn't know what to do afterwards. That was the first time I was able to be proud of someone other than me or Mike.

Stimpson's improvement in practice allowed him to get some time on the field during our second game. It wasn't quite like the first game, but we were definitely ahead by a wide margin. The coaches wanted Stimpson to get some rest as an offensive lineman, but wanted to see what he could do as a defender. After a couple of plays, he was able to record his first tackle. The competitor in me knew that his 1 tackle didn't stand up to my multiple hits, but the captain in me knew that his 1 tackle meant more than my 6.

Chapter 27

The third week started off like a normal week. We started our Monday practice with good stretching. We ended the practice with the coach announcing that Mike and I were to remain starters. Our offensive weapons were looking sharp, and our defenders were looking crisp. We were looking like a team that was going to remain undefeated at the end of the week. On Thursday, even our special team guys were looking like they couldn't be beat. Mike continued to be our kick returner, and showed us during practice why he earned that role. Things were going smooth until Friday. Like sickness or an injury, I never saw it coming and I couldn't do anything about it.

We were playing our first conference game and were ready to start our conference championship run. We were defending the crown and the target was on our back. After two really good tune-up games, we knew we had a sound strategy and a complete team. We even started the game scoring a touchdown. After that, it all fell apart.

I went in the game to play my usual spot. I lined up against the offensive tackle like usual. As soon as the ball was snapped, I stood up and tried getting past the line. That time, however, there were two linemen blocking me. The next few plays had the same result. Even though we were stopping their running back, I couldn't get in to the backfield at all.

When I got back to the sideline, the line coach explained their strategy to me. They saw the way I played the first two games and knew that I was our defensive leader. They also knew that the other guys on the defensive line were decent, but weren't as talented as me. They knew that they would get more success by putting two guys on me, even though it left another one of our guys wide open.

I went back in for the next drive and still couldn't get through. At halftime, and after numerous times of being shut down, I asked the coach if it would be better to bench me. He said there was no way they would bench me because I made a great decoy. From the coach's point of view, having two guys on me left one of our guys able to get into the backfield every time. Even though our guy wasn't talented enough to make a tackle, he was able to put a lot of pressure on the quarterback. If I was benched, they would be at full strength and we ran the risk of nobody getting into the backfield.

We ended up winning that game. I had 0 tackles, but the rest of the defensive line made up for it. Mike scored 3 touchdowns, while our receivers did the rest. For a player looking to get recruited, that game plan would not be conducive. How would I get anybody's attention without any tackles the rest of the season? As a captain, however, it was a great plan. We were getting into the opponent's backfield almost every time. When the quarterback was rushed, he would do foolish things like throw interceptions. The only time we struggled to get into the backfield was during the plays that I was on the sidelines. I found myself involved in an internal emotional battle between the competitor in me and the captain in me.

Chapter 28

For the next five weeks, I was stuck in the same rut. As a starter, I was constantly held up. I wasn't getting the statistics I knew I needed to even be looked at by a major college recruiter. Recruiters were constantly coming to our games, but they were always there for Mike. The table was pretty much set for me; I was a starter, I was a captain, recruits were coming to our games, but I couldn't even produce 1 tackle in a five game span. Knowing that nothing would change no matter what I did, I tried something new.

It was week nine and we were getting ready to face our rivals at West Whitaker. Because we hosted the game the previous season, it was their turn to host that year. After the coach made his usual starting announcements, I pulled him to the side and explained my plan to him. Like I said, I had nothing to lose.

In five weeks of practice, Stimpson had been constantly working on his defensive skills. He was still struggling, but he had come a long way. His skills were increasing, and his speed and strength continued to improve as well. The coach and I both agreed that I was creating a gap in our opponent's offensive line by getting double-teamed. The problem was, whoever found the gap seemed to lack the talent needed to get to the ball carrier in time. It made sense to put Stimpson somewhere in the defensive line. With his speed, he would be able to find, and get through, the gap. Once in the backfield, he would be able to use his strength to take down whoever had the ball. With any luck, West Whitaker would realize that they couldn't leave him open as well, and would possibly call off their double team on me. The coach thought about my plan, and a few minutes later we had a change in the starting defensive line.

During practice the next day, I discussed my plan with the new defensive starter. I explained that his job was to find the gap, get in there as quickly as possible, and tackle the ball carrier as often as possible. Stimpson really liked the idea because he would be able to put his hard work at practice to good use. It would be up to him to change our defensive scheme. Selfishly, I also knew it would be up to him to eliminate my double team problem and put my recruiting chances in a better spot.

On Friday, we were introduced at another pep rally in the gym. Students were decked out in their aqua and dark purple colors. The crowd was intense. We were in a position to give the school their first back-to-back undefeated season and were on our way to the playoffs. Quickly, my excitement was replaced by panic. I discovered that it was my job as a captain to talk to the student body on behalf of the team.

Chapter 29

The last home game of the regular season had a mix of emotions. For us seniors, that game would be our last regular season game. We were also the visiting team in a matchup against our rival school and we were clearly not welcomed. We were one game away from an undefeated season. We were also one game away from an intense playoff run. Personally, I was even more emotionally invested because I knew that game would be my last chance to impress the scouts during the regular season, and I would have to rely heavily on my newly formed plan.

Mike and I got the team together one last time before the game started. I reminded them how important that game was, and how hard we worked to get to where we were. Although the Wolves weren't undefeated, they would surely love being responsible for our only loss. Our team heard the message and continued to build excitement and energy until we all shouted in unison "Go-East-Whit"

Even though West Whitaker was a 30 minute drive, we still had a big section of fans with us. Even cowbell guy and the adult cheerleader made the trek. With the crowd behind us, and our rival across from us, we were ready for war. During the coin flip, we decided to kick off so that we would have the ball to start the second half. That meant our defense would be on the field first and my new plan would take place right away.

Play began. I was on the left side of the defensive line, while my secret weapon was on the right side. West Whitaker always started their games with a run play, so we were expecting one that time. As the ball was snapped, the tackle and the guard both came at me. I tried hard to fight them off, but realized they were their strongest linemen.

That worked out to our advantage because that meant the tackle guarding Stimpson was one of their weakest linemen. That explained why he fell down hard once pushed. With nothing but the ball carrier in front of him, Stimpson not only caught the running back, but he hit him so hard that the ball popped out. West Whitaker was not expecting this and thus, not prepared. They were expecting one of our defenders to be in the area, but they weren't expecting our future all-state offensive tackle to be nose-to-nose with their running back.

They were able to recover the fumble, but they were not able to recover their offensive scheme. With the new twist in the defensive line, they had to either make a quick adjustment, or face that stud defender every time. As was expected, their quick change led to a release of the double team. With two strong defensive ends, we were able to return to the original defensive threat that we had displayed in the first two games of the season.

Selfishly, I wanted to credit our victory to my game plan. Once they had to change their offensive plan of attack, they were never able to recover. I was able to get 4 tackles, while Stimpson got 3 of his own. The truth was, however, that with as many points as our offense put on the scoreboard, West Whitaker didn't stand a chance - no matter what their offensive plan was. That game gave our school its first *back-to-back* undefeated season in school history, and it put our team in a nice place for the playoffs. For me, that game gave me the confidence that I needed as a player, and gave my recruiting hopes another shot at life.

Chapter 30

I took the momentum from the previous week and used it during our playoff run. The first week of practices during the playoffs felt like a whole new season. Due to my slump, I had not been looking forward to playing our Friday night games during the regular season. Who would, after working so hard all week long to end up with no tackles? But once I saw how effective our new defensive plan was, I had life again. Our new defensive end was relieving the pressure I was facing, which allowed me to feel like I could make a difference. During the practices, I knew I was capable of a great game at the end of the week, so I pushed even harder to see it through.

It didn't take long to see of the effectiveness of the defensive change. For the second week in a row, I was able to play like myself again. Just like last year, we knew we would be facing a soft opponent in the first round. Since we didn't lose a game all season, we were playing against a team who barely made it to the playoffs. We still played like it was do or die for us, though. I ended up with a personal best 7 tackles for loss in that blowout; 4 of those came from tackling the quarterback. Mike didn't have quite the game I had, though. Mike managed to break 100 yards, but his only touchdown came from a kickoff return.

During practice in the second round of playoffs, the coach wanted to try something new. We were going to start working on new plays that we hadn't used during the regular season. For some of those to work, Mike had to go from running back to receiver. Needless to say, his catching ability was nowhere near his running ability. To make up for that, rather than running all week in practice, the coach had him practice catching. Mike didn't just play catch with one of the quarterbacks, he had to practice catching the ball while running plays, while running backwards, and even while running with his back to the quarterback. It was ugly to watch at first, but it gradually got better.

Although Mike practiced catching all week, he wasn't used as a receiver at all during the game. I'm pretty sure this had something to do with his lack of talent at catching. His talent at running, however, continued to improve as he scored 3 touchdowns. I didn't have as many tackles as I did the previous week, but my tackle streak did continue. Stimpson was able to add a couple of tackles, as our defense kept their entire offense under 100 total yards. That was probably one of the best victories for our defense. Not only did we stop them from scoring, but we also stopped them from gaining much yardage. Whatever we were doing was working and needed to continue.

We weren't as lucky during the third round of playoffs, as the team we were matched against was able to score 4 touchdowns. We tried our hardest to prepare for that team because we knew they had one of the best quarterbacks in the state, but clearly we weren't as prepared as we should've been. Luckily, their defense wasn't as good as their offense. That game turned into a shootout, giving a victory to the team that scored last. Because of a great coach with great time management, we scored the last points.

That win put us into the semi-finals for the second year in a row. The nerves went away, but the excitement did not. We knew what to expect from that game, but we also knew that that game was the only thing between us and the state finals. We kept our cool though, and kept our heads in the game. Even when we struggled in the first half, we stuck to our game plan of letting Mike run all over the other team, and using our talented receivers to relieve some of the pressure. We also stuck with our strong defensive line that moved like a college football line. Although we went into the locker room losing at halftime, we continued to play like we had played all year. We knew what we were capable of, and we knew that no team could stop us from scoring the 2 touchdowns we would need to win the game. Surprisingly, both of those touchdowns came from our receivers. Our defense stopped our opponents from scoring during the second half, and Mike's punt return towards the end of the game sealed the victory for us.

On the way home from that game, there was a lot for the team to be excited about. We had just spent four weeks sticking to our game plan and beating some of the best teams in the state. We were only one of two teams left in the playoffs. A lot of us felt that we played better as a team that year than we had the previous season. Even though we squeaked by on two of those games, we never gave up, and we played as a solid team. But there was also a lot to be nervous about. The previous year, we made it to the same point. However, that was as far as we got. We faced a team that was bigger, faster, and stronger than us, and they knew our game plan. Unfortunately, we would have to play against that same team again. They were even bigger, even faster, and even stronger than the previous year, and our game plan hadn't changed much since the last time they saw us. Our players were more talented than the previous year, but would that be enough to beat those guys? The one thing I was really curious about was why Mike had been working on catching the ball for an entire month during practice, but never lined up as a receiver during the playoffs. My answer came a few hours later.

Chapter 31

As we got off the bus, the coach pulled the two of us into his office; this time to talk about the upcoming championship game. The coach felt the same way I did. Although our guys grew, theirs did too. He even watched some of their highlights from previous games that season on the way back from the semi-final game and noticed that they were running the same plays as the previous year; the same plays that sent us home as losers. But we did have one advantage that no one was expecting, not even our own players.

During the playoffs, the coach was trying to come up with a way to secretly change our game plan without telling anyone. He knew that if we tried anything out of the ordinary during the playoff games, the defending state champions would pick up on it and would expect it during the finals. He also didn't want to spend practice time preparing for the championship game because he wanted our team to concentrate on one game at a time. That meant he only had a few weeks to come up with a new plan. and only one week to try it out. He wanted my help as the defensive captain to help with the defense plan, and Mike's help as an offensive captain to work with the offensive plan. The plans weren't a major change, but were enough to throw off a team - even a defending state championship team.

Offensively, the other team would be used to Mike as a running back. They knew our offense revolved around him, and shutting him down would shut down our scoring. What they wouldn't expect was a different running back. While Mike was practicing catching, another running back was taking his place at practice. Rather than being a speedy runner, the new guy was a big bruiser that was hard to take down. The new offense would consist of a running back that the opponent wouldn't be expecting, and a new receiver with quick speed. After having improved on his catching, we knew Mike would be hard to beat; once he caught the ball, no one would catch him.

Defensively, the other team was used to the strength, size, and speed of our defensive ends. They would probably put their big, strong guys opposite from us to defend against us. That would put their weaker guys in the middle of the offensive line. They would also probably plan on running up the middle, through our soft defensive tackles, because that was the weak point of our defensive line. The new plan called for switching our defensive ends with our defensive tackles, putting us across from the quarterback. By the time the offense realized what we were doing, they would have to completely change their play calls, and their assignments, during the game. The state finals was not a game where a coach would want to do that.

We spent the entire week working on the new plan. Not only did everyone master it, they loved it. The new running back felt comfortable because he had practiced for so long as a starter. Mike loved the receiver position because it gave him a new, creative way to score touchdowns. We loved it on the defensive line because we kept the initial plan of tackling the guy with the ball, but it put Stimpson and I next to each other and turned us into an immovable force. I personally loved the fact that, for most of the season, I was double teamed and couldn't get past the line of scrimmage. That week in practice, I was the one doing the double teaming, and was able to get past the line of scrimmage every time. I was starting to feel bad for our quarterback getting hit so often.

Just like with the previous year, the entire town of East Whitaker was proud of us. They hung school flags on most of their businesses, and most of the streets were decorated with our school colors. Even though we had already been there once, we were still representing the county on the state's biggest stage. The town was ready to support us, win or lose, and was proud of the fact that we were in the finals for the second year in a row; a feat that had never been accomplished at East Whitaker. We had higher expectations than the citizens of East Whitaker, though. They didn't know about our team's secret. We felt that with our new game plan, we would be coming home winners, and we would be bringing back with us the State of Michigan Football Championship Trophy; a trophy that has never crossed the Becker County line before.

Chapter 32

What a difference a year made. The previous season, we were excited just to make it to the state finals. We were overwhelmed by the fact that we were playing where the Michigan Knights played their games, and had access to a professional football locker room. We were overwhelmed by our opponent and how big they were. One year later, we felt like we were at home. That year, we were there, not just to play in the game, but to win the game. We already knew who are opponent was, and watching them run onto the field filled us with hatred rather than fear. We knew we had something that they didn't have. We knew that our secret weapon was the only chance we had to win.

It was almost humorous watching them on defense. Their defensive line saw a much bigger running back than they expected, but no doubt felt relief when they didn't see one of the state's best running backs behind our offensive line. As they were enjoying what appeared to be an easy day at the line of scrimmage, the defender covering one of our newest receivers started panicking. He began waving his hands in the air and asked for immediate help. Due to his reaction, two other defenders came rushing over and began preparing for a foot chase once they recognized who they were defending. With 11 total players on defense, putting three of them on one of our players obviously left at least one of our players wide open. That one player ran out about 40 yards and wasn't noticed until after he caught the ball and ran it in for an East Whitaker touchdown.

It was even more fun when we were on defense. That's because what we couldn't hear from the sidelines, we could hear on the line of scrimmage. The center, as well as the two guards on either side of him, wear swearing in panic. They knew what we were capable of, and yet never saw it coming. Once the ball was snapped, the only thing they saw was the roof of the stadium as they were all lying on their backs. We didn't get to the quarterback in time, but we sure got to their coach. There wasn't anything he could do other than instruct his quarterback to get rid of the ball quicker.

When we got the ball back a second time, their defense was more prepared for Mike. They knew he had speed, and was a danger on the ground. What they didn't know was how good of a catcher he was. He ran out about 20 yards, then made a sudden cut across the field. The cut was so sharp that he lost his defender. As he ran across the field, the quarterback threw the ball in front of him. Once he grabbed it, he never let go and gave us our second score.

Their second offensive drive led to a touchdown once they were able to regroup and create a drive full of fast moving plays. Even though they were able to score a couple more times, their defense was unable to stop Mike, our new offensive weapon. That took us into the locker room with a small lead at halftime. Once in the locker room, our coach dropped yet another surprise on us. He figured that at halftime, the other team would use the 20-minute break to adapt to our changes. That would've been plenty of time for a defending champion to reconfigure their team, which could've cost us the game. For that reason, the coach wanted us to go back to our original game plan that we had ran all season.

As expected, it worked. When they had the ball, they came up with the solution of putting their strongest guys in the middle of the offensive line in preparation for us. That put their weaker guys on the outside of the offensive line. That also gave Stimpson and I a cleaner path to the quarterback. Within seconds, the quarterback also got to see the roof of the stadium.

Our opponents were also more prepared for us on defense. They were ready for our powerful receiver, who was a danger in the receiving game. In fact, they were so ready that they forgot about our running game and gave up an 80-yard touchdown run that Mike took right up the middle of their defense. By the time their coach figured out our top runner was running again, his decision to go back to their initial game plan was too late, and our lead was too much. We were state champions.

Chapter 33

We've had cafeteria spaghetti and garlic toast many times in our lives, but on that night, it was the best we had ever tasted. That's because, after dinner, we were served a three layer cake of awards, trophies, and records. The coach presented the team with the state championship trophy. It was a beautiful piece of gold that would stay in our school's trophy case forever. It was accompanied by the Becker County Conference Trophy that we also earned that year.

After the trophy ceremony, the coach moved into the records part of the team banquet. Of course, there was no surprise that Mike broke his own record of rushing yards and touchdowns in one season. We were surprised, however, that he broke the conference record in both categories. I was even more surprised to learn that there were more records broken that season. One of our players broke the school record of tackles for loss in one season, and in one game. I had no idea it was me because, for most of the season, I didn't have any tackles. Thankfully, the post-season stats counted as well.

The banquet wrapped up with team awards. These were always fun because it was obvious who some of the recipients would be for some of them, but for others, it was a guessing game. There were five awards handed out that year. The 1st award, the Most Valuable Player of the Season, obviously went to Mike. The offensive strategy was based around him, and none of our opponents out-scored our offense, so it was well deserved. He also deserved the 2nd award, the Offensive Player of the Season, for the same reasons. I was honored, but I kind of predicted that I would take home the 3rd award, the Defensive Player of the Season, after learning that I broke two school records. I also felt honored when the 4th award was announced.

The 4th award was the Most Improved Player Award. That award was given to the player who improved the most in a given season, while being a contributor to the team. I guessed a few names for that one, but didn't get a single one right. I knew it wasn't either of us, since we started the season already improved compared to the previous season. I never considered the winner because I always saw him as the best offensive lineman. However, I never took into consideration his improvement as a defensive lineman. Chris Stimpson went from our worst defensive lineman at the beginning of the season, to a major weapon in our arsenal (and the reason for my record-breaking 7 tackles for loss in one game).

The final award was even more shocking. It was the Shane Hagadorn Inspirational Award, named after an inspirational player from the 1950s. It was awarded to the player that was able to inspire the team to play at a higher level. The coach gave an explanation for the award before handing it out to the recipient. He said that it was the most important award because, without a player to be a role model for the team, we would have a big group of players only looking out for themselves and wouldn't be able to grasp the concept of team work. Without this inspiring player, there's no way we would've earned the state championship trophy on talent alone.

That year's winner started off as a criminal on the street with no athletic ability. After two years, he turned into a leader who was in the weight room every day and became stronger, both physically and mentally. The rest of the team saw how hard he was working, and became inspired to work as hard as he did. Once he became captain, there was no breaking the bond that was created amongst his teammates. That player's hard work and dedication, both on and off the field, was a big reason for winning the trophies sitting in the room that night.

At the end of the night, we were able to take pictures. Many of the pictures included the team surrounding our championship trophies, the two of us with our awards, and pictures of us with our families. On numerous occasions, I've looked at that picture of me holding the Shane Hagadorn Inspirational Award, with my parents on either side, and still can't figure out whose eyes were watering more, my mom's or mine.

Chapter 34

That exciting time of the year finally came. The previous year, Mike went on recruiting trips and had coaches trying to lure him in with luxury. The following year, not only did I have a good chance to live that life, but we would also be deciding on the team that we wanted to play football with for the next four years. We stayed true to our goal of playing college football together. We would only make a decision if it involved both of us. We had just finished an unbelievable record-breaking season, and believed that we had a good chance of achieving that goal. Mike again got offers from the same schools that gave him offers the previous year. They were all anxious for him to play and were not only willing to let him start as soon as possible, but most of them were willing to revolve the offense around him. Sadly, I also got the same offers that year that I had received the previous year; none.

In a private meeting with my coach, I tried to understand why I didn't get recruited. He summed it up that my success simply came too late. Most of the recruiters looked at players during their junior year. Teams started building their rosters with those young athletes in mind. A senior had to really stand out all season long for them to be considered, due to the fact that there was limited room on college football rosters. Unfortunately, all of my big plays came during the playoffs. Even though I had an impressive run, I did not have an impressive overall season. Just like that, our dream was terminated.

I released Mike from our pact. He was left to make a decision on his own. He could sign with any team he wanted without me, or he could join a junior college that would accept me. That decision was made easier when the University of Southern Michigan called him. As usual, he informed the recruiter that he wasn't going to sign without me. That time, however, the recruiter asked to meet with both of us. Suddenly, our plan had a pulse again.

The recruiter agreed to meet with us in our head coach's office. He agreed with our coach that I had a great playoff run, but I would have to have two great years to be considered by most major college football teams. Sadly, that would put Mike in a situation where he would have to play at the junior college level if he wanted to continue playing football with me. If he did that, he would be wasting two years of his football career, would be risking injury, and would jeopardize his chances at playing for a major college, according to the recruiter. Mike's best option was obviously to sign with a major college now, hot off an impressive season, so people would remember his talent and what he did at the high school level. The recruiter made it clear that for the both of us to have any chance at playing together professionally, we would have to play separately at the college level. After he let us digest the bad news, he had good news for us.

He was willing to make an offer that would apply to both of our college careers, and would give us the best opportunity to play together in the long run. The recruiter would talk to a friend of his on the Whitaker Junior College football team. He had a good feeling that they could use my talent. I could then spend those two years, since it was only a two-year program, preparing myself to play at the major college level, and prove that my playoff run wasn't just a fluke. That would give me the best shot at being noticed by the University of Southern Michigan. He couldn't guarantee it, but he was willing to bet that I would be able to make the team with two years of college football experience behind me. That would give us the opportunity to practice together, live together, and be on national TV together for the second half of our college career.

A few days later, the recruiter took the two of us to meet with his friend at Whitaker Junior College. The friend turned out to be the team's head football coach. Surprisingly, he was aware of my career, and was shocked that I hadn't been noticed by any junior colleges in the area. Unfortunately, he never planned for me to visit his school and didn't have room for me on the defensive line. The defensive line slated to start the upcoming season was the same line that took them to the playoffs the previous season, and he obviously wanted to keep them intact. He was able to counter with a better offer, though. If I wanted to stay on defense, I would have to remain a backup defensive lineman during the entire season and wouldn't be able to see much playing time. If, however, I switched to the offensive line, I would stand a better chance at fighting for a starting spot that season because the starting offensive line had some troubled spots.

For me, it had been over a year since playing on the offensive line, but I knew I would still be able to do it. The question was would I be willing to turn my back on the position that I loved so much. After meeting with the coaches, Mike and I went back to my house and talked about our options. Everybody had made good points that day and we knew we would have to be realistic. He didn't want to lose an opportunity with a major college, and I knew that I would have a better chance of starting in the junior college level by being an offensive lineman. Even though I had more fun on defense, would I be willing to sit on the bench for a year? I knew I would have to become a starter as soon as possible to really have any chance of making the University of Southern Michigan's football team.

He reminded me of our promise to make sacrifices in the short-term to achieve our long-term goal. My sacrifice would be walking away from the defensive line, while his sacrifice would be playing without his best friend for two years. Finally, we agreed that we would be willing to play apart for the first two years, if it meant that we could play together the last two. The next day, he officially became a USM Dragon.

Chapter 35

My parents were excited about my decision. Not only was I going to college, but I would still be living at home. Whitaker Junior College was in the city of Whitaker, and didn't have dorm rooms, so living at home was my only option. Mike's parents didn't take the news as well as mine did. They weren't sure if either one of us would graduate high school, so they were very excited to learn that Mike would be going to a top university at no cost to them. What they didn't like was the fact that the University of Southern Michigan was near the Indiana state boarder, five hours away from their home. Because they wouldn't have to pay for his college, Mike's parents bought him a car. However, the car wouldn't be dependable enough for him to make the 10-hour round-trip drive every weekend, so he would only be able to come home during longer school breaks.

With time winding down, we continued to make the most of our spring. Rather than worrying about the two years we would be off on our own, we decided to enjoy the next few months and looked forward to playing together during our junior year of college. We continued to run and spend time in the weight lifting room, and we used our free time after school to work on our grades. We knew that college courses would be more challenging than the high school classes we were taking, so we wanted to prepare ourselves for the next level. Although Mike wouldn't need to maintain really good grades as an athlete at the university, I would have to as a student at junior college. I would especially need to continue working hard on my grades because I would be transferring to USM as a student, not as an athlete, and would need impressive grades to get in.

The studying paid off when graduation day finally came. We ended up fulfilling our promise to our high school coach by improving our grades. We had both started off with a D average but, after two years of hard work, Mike ended up with a C+ average, while I reached a B+ average. We were very proud of how well our grades had turned around, but we were also proud of the simple fact that we were graduating from high school. We'd been in the spotlight before, our names announced over a public address system in front of a large crowd, but that time we couldn't contain our emotions. It wasn't just the 12-year path of school that we were celebrating; we were celebrating a two year journey that turned our lives around forever, thanks to the second chance given to us by a judge. That judge, by the way, was there to watch us accept our diplomas. With him at graduation, we felt like we were finally able to prove to everyone that we didn't take that second chance for granted.

A week after graduation, it was time to say goodbye. Even though we had a three month break before we started our first year of college, Mike would have to leave early to spend the summer working on strength and conditioning with his new team. We decided that we would keep in touch over the phone. I would be curious what the life of a major college football player was like, and what I had to look forward to, while he would be curious about my playing ability at the college level. After talking about our plans for the following two years, there was nothing more to say. Once he got in his car and took off, I was on my own to face the next stage of life.

The College Years

Chapter 36

   It was the first day of summer practice. Because of my grades, I was able to receive a couple of grants from East Whitaker High School. Junior college costs were much lower than university costs, so the grant money was enough to pay for my two years there. Because they would not have to pay for my first two years of school, my parents offered to pay for the second two years if I made it into a university. Because I didn't have to worry about paying for college anymore, I was able to quit my part-time job so that I could focus strictly on football and school. Even though I had already saved a bit of money, I lived a few miles from school, so taking the city bus made more sense than buying a car. Taking the bus also made me feel anxious, though. While playing football in high school, Mike and I would simply walk to the field right after school with our friends on the team. However, all of that changed once I got to college. Suddenly, I had to get to the field by myself, and I didn't know anyone on the field once I got there. After a few stressful minutes, I saw a familiar face. The head football coach I had met during recruiting walked onto the field and got everyone together for our first huddle as a team. Although I had only met the guy once, I knew he wasn't a complete stranger. As he was talking to the team, I decided that I really liked the coach because he treated us like adults, yet knew we were still fresh out of high school.

   Once in the team huddle, rather than going right to work, the coach began to explain how junior college football operated. He knew we were used to watching our favorite college teams on television, but those major college football games had a different format than what we would be a part of. During the regular season, we would play nine games; six of those games would be conference games. At the end of the season, the top four teams in our conference would take part in a conference tournament. After that, all conference tournament winners would be ranked nationally and only the top-14 teams would play in just one post-season game. The top two teams would play in the National Junior College Title Game. The previous year, Whitaker Community College won the Michigan Junior College Conference and was able to play in a post-season game. The coach's goal was to make it to the title game that season.

He began to explain how the season would run. We would spend the summer without pads working on strength and conditioning. A few weeks before the regular season began, we would start practicing with pads. After two weeks, the coaches would decide on their starters. He made it clear that once starters were announced, they weren't permanent positions and could change at any moment. Not only was it up to us to use those first few weeks to make the coaches' decision easier, but it was also up to us to fight to keep those positions once we earned them.

He finally explained his philosophy as a junior college football coach. He knew that all of us were either new to the team and felt like outsiders, or had been on the team for a year and were just starting to form bonds with their teammates from the previous season. He wanted all of us to be on the same page, with no one feeling left out, so he would treat all of us like we were new to the team. He explained that although we were part of a two-year program, some of us would only stay for a year. Since we had a short time together, we would have to quickly form a brotherhood within our team. That being said, he wanted us to use the rest of the day to get to know each other while we did some casual stretching on our own.

Chapter 37

Most of the guys were laughing and having a good time. They were taking advantage of the free time because they knew our practices would get much harder after the first day. Watching those guys, I felt like most of them were playing on that team because they had fun playing football in high school and weren't ready to walk away from it. I wasn't going to let any one of them stop me from achieving my long-term goal. We wouldn't be hitting for a while, so I decided to use my available time to get to know my competition. I wasn't looking to make friends; I just wanted to know who I was up against, and what they were bringing to the table.

I didn't want to waste time on players who I wouldn't be competing with, so I immediately began talking to the biggest guys on the team. The more I talked to them, the more I realized how inaccurate my initial assessment was. Every player I talked to was using junior college as a stepping stone to play major college football. A handful of players were in the same situation I was, but the rest of them were only playing on the team because their grades were too low for major colleges. Even though they were some of the best players in the country, they wouldn't be able to play until they raised their grade point average. That meant that I would be competing with major college level players who all had the same motivating factor as me. My only chance of standing out was to be bigger, faster, and stronger than all of them. As easy as that had been to achieve in high school, it would be hard to do at the junior college level because my new team was full of some of the best high school football players in the state who simply weren't smart enough to get into any major college.

On my way home that night, my anxiety came rushing back. I knew I needed to spend my time on the bus calming myself down. I reminded myself of my first observation at East Whitaker, and how intimidated I was as I watched the fast running backs. That same day, I felt more comfortable once I was able to compare myself to players who would be playing my position. Then I had to remind myself of linemen camp and how I was so obsessed with my competitor that I forgot to accept the reality of both of us starting. Finally, I had to praise myself for using my competition in high school as a motivator, rather than as a reason to run away. That motivation kept me in the starting lineup in high school and helped me become a team captain.

Although I wouldn't be the captain of my team that season, I would again have to use my competitors as motivation to fight for a starting role. It then dawned on me that I would be on the team for two years and shouldn't stress over my first season. I formed a new plan to use the first season as an opportunity to get comfortable with playing at the college level. Playing with guys who were bigger, faster, and stronger than me would allow me to get used to playing with, and against, elite players. I would then work on starting during the next season, knowing that half of my competition would be leaving at the end of the current season and I would have a year of experience by then.

Chapter 38

The next day, I came back to practice feeling more at ease. I felt comfortable being on the field and I no longer felt isolated. I had a goal in mind, and I found it easier to work with a short-term goal, rather than obsessing over the long-term. Once the coach made it to the field, he called us over for a team huddle. In the huddle, he broke down our practice schedule for us. He told us that we would have two months until we started practicing for the regular season. By then, he wanted us to be in the best shape possible, to understand our assigned position, and to memorize the plays that we would be running. Every day for those first two months, we would be working on speed and strength. He would have drills for us to run which would help improve our speed and allow us to make quicker decisions in game-time situations. Due to the heat, we would be doing those drills in the morning. In the afternoons, we would spend time in the weight lifting room where we would be allowed to do our own routines. He felt that since we were all adults, it would be our responsibility to increase our strength on our own. After the first two weeks of summer practices, we would begin trying out for positions. The coach wanted to see what position fit us best based on our size and agility. Finally, we would spend the rest of the summer in our positional groups so that we could memorize plays as they related to our group.

After breaking from the huddle, I quickly planned out how I wanted to use the next two months of summer practices to the best of my advantage. As far as the speed drills were concerned, the only thing I could do was try my hardest, just like I did in high school, working on not being the slowest on the team. I also planned on using the same weightlifting routine that helped me get strong in high school, making sure I didn't waste any lifting time. Finally, I figured memorizing plays wouldn't be that hard as an offensive lineman because my job should be the same in college as it was in high school; stand up once the ball was snapped, and don't let anyone get by me.

After practice, I decided to give Mike a call. I wanted to see how his practices were going, and how he was handling the transition into college football. After we talked, I realized that I had it made compared to him. His strength and conditioning routine was similar. They had the same practice schedule we did, but his workouts were more intense. He was working with the best college football players from all over the country. Competition was tough, so the coaches had to come up with intense drills and practices to determine who the starters would be. The teams they would be playing against were full of elite players as well. That meant they would have to be the strongest and fastest players in their conference in order to win their games. With only one post-season game, and no conference tournaments, every win counted in major college football.

Mike was also disappointed about his chances of starting. When he talked to the recruiter while in high school, it sounded like he would be starting right away. He quickly realized that he wouldn't be able to start until his sophomore year because freshmen usually didn't start their first season. The only way he would've been able to start right away was if he was absolutely the best running back on the team. That wasn't the case because the starter from the previous season was still on the team and he had already earned the trust of the head coach. Unlike junior college, major colleges usually kept the same starters because they already had the experience needed to play at the elite level. Since their running back had been nominated as one of the best running backs in their conference the previous season, USM wanted Mike to use his freshman year to get used to playing at the major college level. After his freshman year, the current starter would graduate and Mike would have a chance at being a starter for the next three seasons.

Chapter 39

For the first couple weeks of summer practice, my plan went off without a hitch. I wasn't the most athletic guy on the team, but I definitely wasn't the weakest. I was able to keep up with the rest of the team during the speed drills, and never finished last. In the weight room, I stuck with my high school routine, and it was paying off. I learned from the other players that a high protein diet would help me gain muscle faster, so I was actually getting stronger faster than I was in high school.

After the first two weeks, it was time to try out for our positions. When we got together for our daily huddle, the coach explained how they were going to determine who played what position. At the major college football level, there was a coach for every position. At the junior college level, however, they didn't have quite the budget, so they simply had a coach for the running backs and receivers, a coach for all linemen, a coach for the defensive backs and linebackers, and a coach for the quarterbacks, who would also double as the offensive coordinator. We were to simply work with the coach for the position that we wanted to try out for. It would be up to that coach if we were talented enough to stay in his group or not. If we didn't make the group, we were asked to work with the special teams' coach, who was also the defensive coordinator, or find our way off the team.

Right away, I found the line coach. It didn't take long to figure out who the four defensive linemen were that the head coach was referring to in our initial meeting. The line coach told us that, unlike in high school, we were allowed to only play on the offensive line, or defensive line, but not both. The head coach had already told me what my chances of playing were if I chose to be a defender, so I went with those going out for the offensive line. There were eight of us on the offensive side and seven on the defensive side. The coach then explained that at the college level, most of his starters would be playing the entire game, so his backups wouldn't see much game time. So even as a backup, I would have to stand out amongst the other backups just to get a decent chance at *some* playing time.

We went through some simple strength and conditioning drills, similar to our familiar high school drills, and at the conclusion were told that we were all talented enough to stay in the linemen group. After reminding us that none of us were declared starters, the line coach told us how impressed he was with our performance, and that we were all in for some good competition. Even though we would be on different sides of the ball, it was important for us to remember that we would all be working as one big linemen group, and he would be our coach for the rest of the season.

Towards the end of the day, our head coach called us in for a quick team meeting. He told us that after the first two weeks of summer practice, our initial group of 80 players had been reduced to 60. Even though we lost quite a few players, the coaches weren't done making cuts. The team only had 55 available spots, so five more players would have to be cut before the regular season began. In an instant, the pressure was on.

Chapter 40

        After a few weeks of stressing, I was able to survive the remainder of summer practices without being one of the five players cut. As I figured, the plays for an offensive lineman were easy to remember. Some of the plays were interesting, though. For some of them, one of the offensive lineman would stand up as soon as the ball was snapped and, instead of blocking, would run behind the center and block on the other side of the line. The shift opened up a gap in our offensive line, but it allowed more coverage for the running back as he ran up the middle of the line. Although those plays were foreign to me, it didn't take long to get the hang of them.

        As the head coach had promised, once the summer practices were over, we had our assigned positions, we all had the plays memorized, and we were all in great shape. Unlike high school, once practice began, it was hard-as-you-can full contact. This allowed us to prove ourselves right from the get. Personally, I didn't waste the opportunity. In our daily huddle, the coach told us that we would be spending the next two weeks in our positional groups. We were to use that time to better ourselves at our positions, and work on our plays as a unit. We wouldn't get together as a big group until we got ready to practice for our first game. Although we wouldn't be able to hit as a team, we were still going full contact in our groups, while being able to show off our speed, as well as our ability to retain information.

        Even though I didn't stand out as one of the best players, I didn't stand out as one of the worst. I quickly learned how different college football was once I struggled to hold back defenders on the line of scrimmage. They made me look weak, but I felt better when I saw that the big defenders were walking over the rest of the offensive line as well. As it turned out, my ability to memorize plays quickly became my biggest weapon. It was the only thing that set me apart from the others who struggled to remember their roles.

After those two weeks, my hard work paid off. Just like the head coach predicted, the defensive line was the same line used the previous season. After struggling to contain them, I wasn't going to argue that decision. The offense had some returning starters as well, but two of the spots went to players new to the team. I wasn't one of those two, but I was the next one called. The three guys who didn't make the starting offensive lineup were designated as a backup center, a backup tackle, and a backup guard; I would be the backup tackle. The coach then went on to explain that even though our backups had designated titles, we still had a backup order, as the titles were only used for the official team roster. So even though I was declared the backup tackle, I would be used to relieve any starter on the offensive line. The coach felt that, of the three of us, I worked the hardest during practice and deserved to be the primary backup offensive lineman. That meant I would be the first one to go into a game if any one of our guys needed a break. Suddenly, my chances of impressing the University of Southern Michigan skyrocketed; it was up to me to keep my position, and I was more than motivated to fight for it.

That night, I talked to Mike to see how his summer practices had turned out. He told me that he was the number two running back on the team. He wasn't the starter, but he would definitely get some good playing time. At Southern Michigan, the starting running back ran most of the plays, while the backup running back would play if the team was close to the goal line. He knew that I wouldn't be able to watch the games on television, since our games were at the same time, but he wanted to make sure I recorded them so that I could actually watch him play on national TV. I then told him my good news; I had become the number one backup offensive lineman on a college football team.

Chapter 41

It was finally time to practice as a whole team. In our daily huddle, the coach told us that we would be spending the week getting ready for the upcoming game. Although it would be used as a tune-up game, it was still a game to be taken seriously because it counted towards our overall record. He reminded us that even though starting positions had been announced the previous week, those positions weren't guaranteed until game day, and we would have to spend that week fighting to retain those roles.

The team we were scheduled to play wasn't quite the tune-up game I was used to in high school. The way I saw at it, it was a tune-up game for the other team. Their team didn't make it to the title game the previous season, but they were ranked as the number three overall junior college football team. They lost a few players during the off-season, but they still had the same coach who clearly knew what he was doing. We were definitely the underdogs. But, as our coach explained, every team had a 0-0 record in the first week of the season, so we were all tied for first place.

Even though I wasn't a starter, I made it my goal that week to make the coaches feel comfortable with me as the number one backup. I had a rough week the previous week by letting the defensive line through me, but once I knew what to expect, it happened less and less frequently in practice. Although I didn't stop them every time, I held them up more than any other backup lineman on our team.

The rest of the week went by fast. Unlike high school, though, we had five days of practice instead of the four that I was used to. The practice schedule was pretty much the same as what I had done before, only we used the additional day to spend more time working with the entire team. The biggest difference by far was the level of intensity. Because we were all fighting for a chance to be in the spotlight, we were treating practices like games. Everybody went full blown and wouldn't stop until told to do so by the coach. We all wanted to play for major colleges, and everyone knew they only had two years to prove their abilities at this level. Even though I was a tough blocker, I still didn't stand out as the best on the line. Knowing my memorization skill was my biggest asset, I continued to focus on that and made sure that I was the only one on the line hitting all the right blocks - *every time*.

Towards the end of the week, I thought my chances of starting were getting much better. One of the offensive starters messed up on a play and ended up falling to the ground. I knew that because the game was one day away, it would be too late for the coaches to switch starters, but they would've been forced to if the guy couldn't get back up. As it turned out, he missed the block because he hurt his right ankle, and it was the pain that made him fall to the ground. I felt relief for him when he got back up on his own, and yet, was discouraged when he went in for the next play. Just like I would've done, he continued to play through the pain.

Chapter 42

I wasn't nervous about playing time, I was nervous about the game itself. I was used to high school games, but I didn't know what to expect from a college football game. I had a feeling it would be intense based on practice. And I knew the intensity of practice was nowhere near what I would be facing during the game. I once again had that uncomfortable feeling of not quite belonging.

That feeling went away once I looked up at the stands on game day. I was used to playing in front of a sold out crowd on Friday nights. After seeing massive college arenas with standing room only on television, I was shocked when I saw that the stands were nearly empty during our Saturday afternoon game. Apparently, junior college football games weren't a big draw. It didn't help that the University of Northeastern Michigan was playing 30 minutes away. Even our stadium was unimpressive. It reminded me of our practice field at East Whitaker. There wasn't much to it; a one-level press box, three sections of bleachers on either side of the field, a run-down score board, and an eight foot long table used to sell snacks to fans.

Once the angst of playing college football went away, I was able to concentrate on the game. I was on a team of really tough guys, playing against another team of really tough guys, who shared the common goal of victory. All we had to do was score more points than they did. I had the simple goal of protecting my quarterback; it was a goal that I had become very familiar with.

After three quarters of play, the game remained close. In college, the quarter lengths were three minutes longer than what they were in high school, so a lot of the new guys were starting to get tired. I was fine with that because I figured eventually one of our guys would tire enough to require a break. Unfortunately, those guys were so obsessed on impressing recruiters that they were willing to play on. I did, however, get my chance to play towards the end of the 4th quarter.

It seemed the pain became too much for the lineman who had injured himself a few days ago during practice. After being pushed around too many times, his ankle finally gave. I was called in to take his place at the tackle position. Quickly, my fears came back. That would be my first play as a college football player and it would gage if I was ready to take on the world of college football.

Once the ball was snapped, I stood up quickly. Waiting for the snap was no longer an issue of mine. As the defender attacked me, I realized that he wasn't as strong as our starting defenders; the ones I had battled in practice. After a few seconds of blocking, I was ready to take him on again for the next play. This time, once the ball was snapped, he used his speed to elude me and found his way to our quarterback. I was disappointed that I couldn't prevent our quarterback from getting sacked. I was devastated when the coach called me out of the game.

The guy who took my spot was able to stand his ground against the defense for the rest of the drive. Although we didn't score the game winning touchdown on that drive, we would get another chance after our defense finally shut them down. As expected, my replacement went back in to finish the game. Even though we lost that game, I was selfishly more upset that I lost my spot.

When I got home from the game that night, I watched with my parents in the living room as the

University of Southern Michigan played their first game of the season. As Northeastern fans, we wouldn't have been caught dead rooting for USM. But that night, we weren't rooting for the Dragons; we were rooting for their backup running back, Michael Upton. In the 1st half of the game, Mike was able to score his first college touchdown. Once USM was up by four touchdowns, he was able to play out the rest of the game. He tallied 2 more touchdowns and 100 yards of rushing. I knew it wouldn't be long until he became a legend there, too.

Chapter 43

We gave each other a day to take in our first college football experience. For Mike, he needed time to celebrate. For me, I needed time to get over it. The next day, enough time had passed and we were ready to talk about our experiences. Although they were nearly opposite, we definitely had stories worth telling.

Mike loved every minute of his big day. The locker rooms were gorgeous, and the stadium was enormous. The attendance was nearly 70,000, and they were all wearing Dragon red and black. Rather than being nervous, he was excited for the game. He knew what he was doing, and he was one of the best at it. Mike was very comfortable with his position, and knew it wouldn't matter how much stronger the opponent was as long as they couldn't catch him. When he scored his first touchdown, it wasn't as challenging as he thought; all he had to do was run the ball in 10 yards. When he got a chance to play more, he took advantage of how tired the other team was. He even liked the fact that he wasn't returning punts or kickoffs because it allowed him more energy as a running back. Finally, he accepted that he wouldn't be a starter that season, but he was no longer anxious about playing college ball.

After I shared my depressing story, he told me he was already aware of my disappointment. Even though our games weren't televised, they were still broadcasted over the radio. He was upset when he heard what happened, but he knew that I would use the experience as more fuel for the fire. Mike knew I couldn't let it get me down, and I would instead use it as motivation to keep it from happening again. After we talked, I felt better about my game and was ready for the next week.

That next day, the dread came rushing back. After getting through my first game of college ball, I was faced with my first day of college courses. My grades had gotten better over the years, but I knew college would be a bigger challenge for me. I was expecting rooms of 300 students trying to keep up with the professor, as they quickly went through their lecture. As soon as I walked into the room, my anxiety disappeared.

The math room looked just like a high school classroom. There were 15 tables that comfortably sat two students each. I didn't know what I wanted to do when I grew up, so my plan at junior college was to take basic classes. I would then pick a major once I got to the University. That meant I had a semester full of introductory courses. After skimming through the syllabus, I had a feeling that the homework load would be a lot less than it was in high school. I developed good study habits in high school, so it seemed like college could possibly be less challenging.

I was more relieved as the professor introduced himself. As it turned out, the guy was teaching the class as a hobby. He was an accountant, so teaching math was more of a way to keep his brain challenged. He encouraged the 25 of us to take good notes because we would be allowed to use our notes during the three course exams. Then, after meeting with us for an hour, the class was dismissed. My next two classes were also scheduled to last an hour, but we were dismissed even earlier than that. After less than three hours of lecture, my first day as a college student was over. Why couldn't my first game have gone that well?

Chapter 44

As expected, my screw up during the game didn't get swept under the rug; nor did it get a private meeting with the coach. Instead, I was used as an example of how easily our roles could be taken away from us. After one bad play, I was replaced by another player. I wasn't given a second opportunity, rather I gave someone else a first chance. That person ended up making the most of his opportunity because our starting tackle wouldn't be playing that week due to his injury. I did get my role reinstated as lead backup, but I would've been starting that week if it weren't for my fatal error during the game.

As Mike predicted, I used that embarrassment to improve myself as a player. I got a taste of what it felt like to be taken out of a game. I also got a taste of what it felt like to play college football. Even though it had the feel of a scrimmage, I liked playing much better. Once I got that taste, I would do whatever it took to get more of it. I made sure I wouldn't lose my spot again, and I worked even harder against our defenders. Just like the previous week, I was not able to stop them every time. I did, however, hold them back more times than they got past me.

My work didn't just improve on the practice field, either; it also improved in the weight room. I knew I would have to be stronger if I wanted to stay on the offensive line, but I knew I would also have to be faster. The guy that got by me during the game took advantage of our difference in speed. I knew I would have to improve my speed if I didn't want that to happen again. I actually extended my weight room time to spend more time on the treadmill, even though I was already doing the speed drills during practice.

I was willing to put my body through torture if it meant more playing time on Saturdays.

I also used that week to get adjusted to the new challenge of balancing school and practice. Even though the days were shorter, and the work was easier, I would have to work harder on my grades than I did in high school if I wanted to transfer to a University. I would need at least a 2.0 grade point average, on a scale of 1-4, to be able to transfer, but I wanted to better my chances by maintaining at least a 3.0 average. I would have to spend even more time studying, in addition to the extra time on the treadmill. Slowly, college was becoming overwhelming again.

Chapter 45

The following game was our second non-conference game, but our first away game. I hoped that at least our away games would be a little more luxurious than high school (after all, we were representing an entire college). I realized how wrong I was when the bus arrived. Only one bus was used to take our team of 55 to the game. I would not have been surprised to learn that my parents had used the same bus when they went to college many years ago. The once-white bus was no longer white, and the step leading into the bus had been rusted through. I feared that we would start the season on a losing streak because we wouldn't be able to make it to the game. To my relief, we arrived in one piece.

As the game went on, the new offensive tackle continued to secure his role. I knew eventually he would have to mess up, though. As the 2nd quarter began, he proved me right. The play he ran called for him to stand and quickly run to the other side of the line to block for the running back. It was one of those tricky plays, but it was a play that we had worked on numerous times during practice. When the ball was snapped, the guy quickly stood up, ran to the other side of the line, then stood there and looked for someone to block. He ran the play flawlessly, but unfortunately, he ran the wrong play. Once he left his spot, their defender met our running back and took him down hard. Our running back didn't expect the lineman to leave, so he was surprised when he met the defender early. In fact, he was so surprised that he fumbled the ball.

The next time our offense went out there, our team would be using a different offensive tackle. I knew I would only have one chance to prove my worth. I guess my extra time on the treadmill paid off because no one got past me during that drive. I was expecting some praise from our line coach after the drive was over, but I guess that kind of performance was more of an expectation in college. At least it was good enough for me to finish the game on the field.

After the game was over, I was again more concerned with my performance than the result of the game. We won the game, but more importantly, I didn't let anyone past me. I tried using the bus ride back home to enjoy the feeling I had after my redeeming performance, but I couldn't even hear myself think. On that trip, I learned the impact a bad muffler had on a moving vehicle.

As it turned out, Mike had produced another great game. Even though he was a backup, he was quickly gaining popularity after only playing in two games. He was known to all the students, and even the professors would talk about his game performance during class. He was invited to the best parties, and became popular there, too. As much fun as he was having during his first season, he knew he would only get better and the parties would only get bigger.

Chapter 46

After another good day of school began the week, I was really looking forward to practice. With our tackle still injured, and a great personal performance during the game, there was no way I wouldn't be a starter in our third game. After the daily huddle, we went to work with our small groups. As more time went by, the more nervous I became. I knew the news would come, I just didn't know when. A few minutes into group practice, I got some news, but it wasn't the news I was looking for.

The coach announced that I would remain the number one backup for the offensive line. He also announced that our injured tackle simply sprained his ankle and he would be good to go at the end of the week. I was crushed. I finally earned a spot on the starting line, just to have it taken away again. At least I had a good spot amongst the backups. It would still be up to me to earn more playing time during the upcoming games.

As the season went on, I retained that number one backup spot. I didn't see much playing time, but when I did get in to play, I made the most of it. In the next six games that followed, I didn't let a single defender by me. Unfortunately, the starting offense remained flawless as well, so I remained the top backup. A big help in retaining that spot came from my improved speed and strength. I continued my intense workout routines throughout the season, and spent more and more time on the treadmill.

Mike continued to improve his season as well. He was still considered a backup running back, but he played almost as much as the starting running back. The coach was really impressed with his speed and his knack for finding the end zone. He didn't want his new running back to waste his talent sitting on the bench, so he decided to alternate running backs in an effort to throw off the opponent's defense. And even though they pretty much split playing time, he still led his team in both rushing yards and touchdowns.

Another surprise during my first season of playing college football was the possibility of not making it to the playoffs. In high school, your team simply had to have more wins than loses to make the cut. In junior college, we would have to be one of the top four in our conference just to advance to the conference playoffs. We had more wins than losses, but we were only tied for 4th place going into the last game of the regular season. We would need a victory in order for Whitaker Junior College to avoid being kept out of the playoffs for the first time in five seasons.

Chapter 47

As with the rest of the games that season, I hardly got a chance to play in the last regular season game. Even though I was only a part of a few plays during that game, I was still a part of a team that was going to fight their way into the playoffs. Finally, with the game over, we walked off the field as victors.

Actually, we didn't walk off the field, we ran off. We had been tied for 4th place. We didn't just need to win; the team we were tied with had to lose. That team was Faith Community College, a team that beat us on our home field during week five. It was explained to me that for us to make it to the playoffs, we would have to have a better record than Faith at the end of the season. If we had the same record as they did, Faith would make it to the playoffs because they had already beaten us. As luck would have it, FCC played their game right after ours finished. As a team, we ran into the locker room to watch their game in the hopes that they would lose and give us the better record.

Faith Community College was playing Byron Junior College. Byron was the best team in our conference, and had already secured their spot in the conference playoffs. Even though they would be number one in the playoffs, no matter what the outcome of the game was, they would still be trying their hardest to win so that they would have a better national rank while trying to make it into the National Junior College Title Game. We looked forward to watching the game, knowing that there was no way FCC would take the victory from Byron Junior College.

The game started out as a blowout. Going into halftime, Byron was up by 21 points, and we were on the verge of securing our place in the conference playoffs. During the 2nd half, Byron decided to play their backup players to save their starters for the following week. That would prove to be a major mistake. Faith Community College was able to fight their way back into the game. Going into the 4th quarter, Byron was only up by one touchdown. But after their punt returner fumbled the ball near the goal line, FCC was able to take advantage and tie the game up.

Our chances of making it to the conference playoffs came down to the last few minutes of that game. With possession of the ball, a score from Byron would open the way for us to play in the playoffs. If, however, FCC stopped them and came up with a score of their own, Whitaker Junior College would be out of the playoffs, breaking their 5-year streak. The next play was one of the most painful plays to watch as a spectator. Byron's running back got the ball with time running out and nothing in front of him but the end zone. We were guaranteed to play the following week - until a line judge declared that the running back had stepped out of bounds as time had expired.

That day, I learned about college football overtime rules. Junior college used the same rules as major college football. Each team was given the ball at the opponent's 25-yard line. After each team had a chance to score, the team with the most points in that period won. If both teams scored the same amount of points, they would move on to another period until one team was able to score more than the other at the end of a round. After two periods, Faith Community College came up with the most impressive, and most heartbreaking, comeback I had ever seen, both as an athlete and as a spectator.

Chapter 48

The next few weeks were dedicated to school. Thanks to a surprising performance by Faith Community College, I spent my first post-season in three years following the playoffs as a spectator rather than as a player. Since we were out of the playoffs, our coach had no use for us until summer practices started back up the following season. He wanted us to enjoy the break and use the time to let our bodies heal. I took his advice and enjoyed the time, but I did not let my body heal. Instead, I continued with my intense weight lifting, as well as speed drills on the treadmill. I figured that if everyone else took the coach's advice, then I would be the only one in the weight room during the off-season, which would give me a huge advantage. When I wasn't working out, I was using my extra time to study and complete homework assignments. The only time I gave myself a break was when the University of Southern Michigan was playing on TV.

As a fan of the sport, Mike was fun to watch. Any time he had the ball, he could turn the play into magic. As his best friend, it was still hard to believe that he was the same guy I witnessed running from the Becker County deputies a few years back. The guy I grew up with was a star on national television. He wasn't the best performer on the team, nor was the team built around him, but I had a strong feeling that he had a lot to do with their 10-1 record going into their last game of the regular season.

Their last game was an important game. Even though they had only lost one game, their record still wasn't good enough to play in the Major College Football Championship Game. They were, however, trying to play for another prestigious post-season game. Other than the national championship game, the top four prestigious college games were played on New Year's Day. The only thing keeping USM from playing on January 1st was a battle with their rival, and our hometown team, the University of Northeastern Michigan. It was a game that divided the town of Whitaker. Half of the town would root for UNM because you could practically see their campus from Whitaker City Hall. The rest of the town would root for their hometown hero on the rival team. Either way, nobody planned on missing that game, and not a seat was available in Becker County Stadium.

Chapter 49

A few days before the rivalry game was set to kickoff, Mike gave me a call. He couldn't stop talking about how excited he was to come back home and play in front of his friends and family. It would also be interesting for him because he grew up rooting for Northeastern, but he was trying to be part of a team that beat them. Once he caught his breath, he gave me even better news. The students were allowed a certain amount of tickets to go to the game and represent the visitors' cheering section. He was able to grab two of those tickets, and planned on giving them to his parents so that they could watch him play. As he was getting those tickets, his parents were getting tickets of their own, so he was left with two extra tickets to the game. He knew I would want one of them, but he didn't know what to do with the other. My parents never missed one of my games, so it was an honor to take my dad to our first major college football game.

I went through many experiences as a high school football player, and it was fun to go through those experiences with my best friend. That Saturday, I was able to enjoy a new experience with my dad. To enjoy the full experience, my dad and I parked in the shuttle lot. The shuttle lot was a parking lot used for partying and tailgates prior to the game. Buses would run every few minutes to take fans from the parking lot to the game at no charge. It was fun to park with the other fans and ride to the game in a bus full of rowdy college kids.

When the bus dropped us off, we were standing in front of Becker County Stadium. I've seen it on TV numerous times, but in person, the stadium was the biggest thing I had ever seen in my life. The walls were so tall that my neck hurt as I was attempting to look up to the top. Once inside the stadium, we were greeted by a sea of fans traveling from left to right. We had no idea where we were going, but it was so busy that we didn't have time to stop for directions. We simply jumped in with the crowd and looked to the ceiling for our section number.

The stadium held nearly 60,000 fans, 10,000 less than Southern Michigan's stadium. About 50,000 of those fans were wearing the colors of Northeastern Michigan. Spread throughout the crowd were the other 10,000 fans wearing black and red. UNM had a record good enough for a post-season game, but it wouldn't be a very prestigious one. However, it was a rivalry game, so the fans were going to support their team as much as possible to beat their cross-state rival. I chose to be unbiased and wore my college uniform to the game. I wanted to root for Mike as a player, but I wanted to root for Northeastern as a team. Either way, I was just glad to be there.

Our section number took us to a smaller tunnel that led inwards towards the field. As I looked ahead, I could start to see the field. The more we walked up the tunnel, the more I could see. Finally, we were at the end of the tunnel and I could see everything. After finding our seats, I got a chance to soak it all in; It was breath taking. The scoreboard was crystal clear and had a large television built into it. It allowed the fans to watch the game, while keeping track of game statistics. The grass was bright green, and the field well maintained. Once the overwhelming feeling was gone, I was ready to watch a great game. A few minutes later, that overwhelming feeling came back.

As both teams made their way on the field, I was able to see how much bigger, and stronger, major college football players were. On television, they seemed like they were the same size as the guys I was used to playing against, but in person they were much larger. As I sized up my future competition, I saw a familiar face. There he was, in his red and black, the future star of the team.

I had seen all of his season games on TV, but that day was his best game by far. I don't know if it was due to the post-season being on the line, the energy of playing a rivalry game, or the fact that we were there in his corner, but something gave him extra fire power. That performance gave USM their 11th win of the season, and a ticket to play on New Year's Day.

Chapter 50

Once the game was over, I was able to meet up with Mike. He was about to board the team bus when he saw his parents, my dad, and I coming towards him. He was bragging about his game, but he was even more excited that we showed up as promised. He boasted that he stepped up his game because he knew we were there. He also wanted to show the University of Northeastern Michigan that they made a mistake in not offering the both of us scholarships. After our very brief conversation, we wouldn't see him again until Christmas break.

While he was home on break, we spent a few days hanging out together. Both of our schools gave us three weeks off, but Mike was only in town for a week because he had to get ready for his post-season game. One of those days, while hanging out at the mall, I was able to share my grades with him. I made it through my first semester of college and had just finished my final exams. When all of my grades were in, my transcript was sent to my house. I had managed a 3.75 grade point average. He enjoyed my surprise, then smiled because he had a surprise for me too; he presented me with an all-expenses paid trip as a recruit to watch his post-season game in Wyoming. I could hardly wait for that day to arrive.

On the day of the journey to the Wyoming game, I was asked to first check in with the recruiter at the Southern Michigan stadium. From there, I boarded one of the team buses with a small group of high school students. The USM recruiter we met the previous year was on the bus and explained to me that the reason I was being treated as a new a recruit was that they were still interested in me playing on their team in a few years, so they wanted to give me the same experience that they would give any other high school recruit; a trip on the luxury bus, a plane ride with the team, a bus ride to the stadium, and a field pass to watch the game on the sidelines. While on the plane, I felt like Mike must have felt when he was being recruited by those numerous universities. Although he was making the same trip I was that day, we rode on different buses, and I was in a different section of the plane. Even on the field, I was in an area reserved just for recruits.

Watching the game in the stadium was similar to the time I watched it with my dad. I wasn't too overwhelmed by being on the field because I was used to that. I was, however, amazed with the Dragons' entrance. For all New Year's Day games, both teams were allowed to enter the stadium the same way they would as if they were playing at home. Maine State University simply ran onto the field as soon as their fight soon began to play. The dragons' entrance was different, though. As soon as they were ready, the indoor stadium went dark. I could barely make out a large statue being dragged out from the concourse and placed in front of the player's tunnel. The statue then lit up and looked just like the head of a dragon. The dragon was black and had bright, red eyes. The eerie dragon opened its mouth and a large ball of fire came out, soon replaced by smoke. From the smoke emerged the University of Southern Michigan dragons. My heart was pounding.

Chapter 51

They ended up losing their post-season game and eventually became the number nine team in the country. Even though Mike was disappointed, he was looking forward to the next season because he would be the clear starter. Just like me at the end of my season, he found more free time without football. He would have two months to himself before spring practices began. Unlike me, however, he used that time to let his body heal. He was already on a major college team, and was sure to get the starting position. He didn't want to risk injury by pushing it too much. He also didn't worry about his grades because he was maintaining a 2.5 grade point average, which was just over the 2.0 average needed to stay in school as a student-athlete.

During the spring, his team ran a team scrimmage. At the scrimmage, their potential starting offense, with their potential backup defense, would play against their potential starting defense, with their potential backup offense. This gave their coaches a chance to run new plays and see if they felt comfortable with their proposed starters. Mike was on the starting offense during the scrimmage, and the coaches seemed happy with their decision.

Our team couldn't run a scrimmage because our team was too small. We would only be able to scrimmage with the guys returning to the team from the previous season and couldn't use our high school prospects. About half of our guys were leaving that year, which left us with 30 players for the new season. Mike's school, on the other hand, had a four-year program, so they had about 60 returning players.

Because we had the spring off, the coaches allowed us to practice on our own. They didn't have enough players to run official practices, but we were allowed access to the field, use of the weight room, and use of any of the team equipment that we needed. Those practices were fun because we ran them as players, and there wasn't any pressure. The level of intensity was lowered because no one wanted to risk injury, but the level of activity was consistent with regular practices. Those practices allowed me to settle down and actually enjoy playing for once, rather than stressing out about starting. That would wait for a few months once the summer practices began.

After the spring, my second semester of school was over. We both had maintained the same grade point averages we'd had in our first semester. I was proud of my grades and knew I was definitely going to be able to transfer to USM as a student. With school over for the year, Mike was able to enjoy a two week summer break before jumping back into practice. We spent that time just like we did at Christmas break. As Mike left for his second year, he pointed out that I was already halfway done with junior college. That season would be my last season to display what I had learned at the college level. He would continue to sell me to the recruiter, but it was up to me to improve as a player.

Chapter 52

We were given a long time to recover, but the time still went by fast. After the short summer break, it was time for our hot August practices to begin. When the bus dropped me off, I felt more at home than I had the year before. I even laughed at myself when I remembered how I had felt the previous season. As I walked onto the field that time, I saw many familiar faces. I knew what the summer practices had in store for me, and I knew that the first day of practice would be my last day to actually enjoy myself until the season concluded.

As the coach called us over for our first team huddle of the season, I expected the same lecture he gave us the previous year. Again, he told us how junior college worked, the schedule for the season, and his personal philosophy. This year, however, he wasn't going to leave it up to another team to decide our playoff fate. He, instead, wanted us to make it to the playoffs on our own by winning more regular season games. For most of us, we were fired up; for the new guys, they were still anxious and didn't know what to expect. They seemed to relax when the coach gave us the rest of the day to meet and greet.

Unlike the previous year, I used that day as suggested by the coach. I already knew who my competition would be and I knew what I would have to do to become a starter. Even though I was next in line to be a starter a season ago, I realized that I was entering a new season and I would have to start all over in proving to the coaches just how valuable I could be to the team. My memorization skills improved, I had the strength needed to stop defenders, and I had the speed to keep them from eluding me. But this season, I had one big weapon that I didn't have the previous season; experience in playing college football.

I spent the next two weeks with the team working on strength and endurance. That year, I was able to begin the season with the same intense workout routine that I developed halfway through the previous season. I could tell that my speed and strength had increased. I felt as if I was standing out a bit more than the other guys.

After two weeks, we tried out for our positions. I already knew my role on the team, so I didn't hesitate in walking over to the line coach once we broke from team huddle. That season, one of the new guys wasn't quite ready to make it as a lineman. He was too slow to get off the line so he was given the option of trying out for the special teams or leave the practice field. He never came back.

Once in our groups, I learned that we would be running the same plays as the previous year. That gave me the advantage of already being familiar with the plays. It finally made sense why last season's starters consisted of guys who had played the previous season; practice was much easier the second time around. That meant that all I had to worry about was increasing my strength, my speed, and my ability to compete against the other linemen.

During summer practices, we spent two months working as a team to get ready for the upcoming season. We were all in great shape, we had our positions, and we had most of the plays memorized. Our team was ready for the regular season. We were playoff bound.

Chapter 53

As summer practice ended, the intensity increased in season practice. We went back to those practices with pads and vengeance; 55 players had to fight their way to fill 24 roster spots. In our offensive line group, eight players would be fighting for five available positions. Even though three of us were returning from the previous season, we still had to earn our place. It was time to use my weight room time, my treadmill time, and my study time on the practice field to my advantage.

As a group, we pretty much had the same athletic ability. None of us were overly faster, or stronger, than anyone else. Once again, I would not be able to stand out athletically. My biggest weapon, for a second season, would have to be my ability to memorize plays. Only three of us were able to run most of the plays flawlessly.

As the two weeks of pre-season practice went on, my uncertainty began to increase. I could feel myself improving, but I wasn't sure if the coaches noticed. I knew that I couldn't spend another year as a backup lineman because I would then end up with very little playing time over two seasons and would not be able to impress the University of Southern Michigan. In an effort to calm my nerves, I gave Mike a call.

He was waiting to hear the official word on his starting status as well. Even though he had an impressive run the previous season, and the running back that split the work load with him had graduated, he still wasn't sure if he had done enough to impress the coaches. After hearing his news, I got even more depressed. I was hoping for a pep talk to cheer *me* up, but instead, he was going through the same emotions I was going through. I encouraged him to look at his situation from a coach's point of view.

Last year, he came to the team as a freshman. Right away, he earned his place as a backup running back. As a backup, he earned himself more playing time and scored the most touchdowns on the team. A season later, he was coming back with a year of experience, and without experienced competition. The coaches would be foolish to start someone else.

As I heard the words coming out of my mouth, I realized that they also applied to my situation. Somehow, counseling him calmed me down as well. I was right, though; the coaches would be foolish if they started someone over me. I fought hard for a season, and was fighting even harder for another. I was ready to give it my all for the next few months.

The next conversation we had a few days later was much brighter. As expected, they made Mike a starter. He would be the only starter in his position for the team and would not have to split carries with anyone else. I, too, was named a starter. After a season of hard work, my short-term goal of starting by my second year was achieved; I was the starting right tackle for Whitaker Junior College.

Chapter 54

The following week in practice began like any other week. After our daily huddles Monday and Tuesday, we went to work in our small groups. In our linemen group, we continued to work on our plays and our timing off the snap. I didn't feel any different as a starter and continued to target the game at the end of the week. Practice later in the week, however, changed.

Wednesday was a day used to work with the whole team. On those days, we scrimmaged against each other in preparation for the upcoming game. During those scrimmages, I worked with the starting offense. It finally hit me that I was really starting, and I suddenly had a different feel for practice. In the first two days of the week, I was so used to our schedule, that I got too comfortable with practices. However, once I remembered the position I was in, I snapped out of it and began to block like a starter.

As practices went on that week, our defense found it hard to get by me. Though they weren't the same big bruisers from the previous season that I struggled against, they were just as tough. Even in practice, I made sure that no one got past me because I knew I needed to protect not only my quarterback, but my starting role as well. I hadn't had the easiest time so far in my football career, so losing my starting spot two days before the first game was very realistic.

I felt more relaxed once we made it to our final Friday practice. It was a practice used mostly to make sure our special team guys knew what they were doing, and a practice where we didn't have to wear pads. More importantly, this practice meant that nobody else had an opportunity to take my spot; it was mine alone. My name would be in the program and would be announced over the loud speaker during the game, assuming our out-of-date field still had a working loud speaker system.

As practice let out, I was flagged down by the head coach. He congratulated me on earning my spot. He wanted me to know that he knew about my long-term goal of playing professionally, and how hard I had been fighting to make sure I achieved it. After reminding me that the opportunity to be a starter was mine to lose, he informed me of the proud tradition of sending players on to major colleges from junior colleges. At the junior college level, coaches weren't just judged by records, playoffs, and post-season games; they were judged by how many players they sent to the next level. He insisted that if I continued to fight hard all season and never slowed down, I would end up giving him his next bragging right.

Chapter 55

Finally, it was game day. I had spent a year getting ready for that moment, but it was well worth the wait. I finally made it onto a college playing field as a starting offensive lineman. The team was excited because it was the first game of the season; I was excited because it was the first day of a rewarding season. To add to my excitement, as well as wear on my nerves, I had to begin that game by watching from the sidelines since our opponent had the ball first. After a good stop from our guys, it was finally my time to shine.

I went into the huddle as a starting tackle on the right side of the line. The play was a simple run play up the middle to test out their defense, but I knew I had the hard task of allowing my running back to get the ball safely and gain a couple of yards without being tackled in the backfield. If I let the defender through, he would get tackled, but more importantly, I would've failed. I wasn't ready to do that, especially not on my *first* play.

As the ball was snapped, I stood up and got ready to block. Just like in our scrimmages, there was a defender right in front of me. When I put my hands up to block, his body went down. On my first play as a starting offensive lineman at the college level, not only did I do my job correctly, but I did it well. I knocked the guy down. I didn't knock him down every play, but not once did the defense get past me.

As the game was moving along, I began to appreciate the difference between playing football as an offensive lineman and as a defensive lineman. As a defensive lineman, my goal was to get to the ball carrier. Although the goal never changed, the challenge was finding new ways to get into the backfield while avoiding the offensive lineman. Once in the backfield, I was rewarded with the opportunity to hit someone as hard as I could. However, as an offensive lineman, my goal was to stop the defender from getting past me. Even though the defensive line made slight adjustments for each play, my goal, again, was always the same and achieving that goal was accomplished by simply standing up and blocking. If I did a good job, I kept playing; if I did a bad job, I sat on the bench. In short, the life of an offensive lineman was boring and not very rewarding. Although it would be a psychological struggle to maintain my enthusiasm all season, I found the role physically achievable and no one got past me that entire game.

After our first win of the season, I started to regret my decision of choosing to play on the offensive line the previous season. I was clearly good at what I did, but I was almost getting bored with it. If I would've chosen defense my first season, I would've had more fun. I then remembered the big difference between having fun and being a starter. If I stayed on defense, I wouldn't have been able to start that first season, and may not have gotten a chance to start my sophomore year. As a starting offensive lineman, however, I was given a starting role on a college football team, which gave me a much better chance of moving on to play football for a major college team. With that comparison in mind, I never regretted my decision again.

Chapter 56

The first day of school went by easier than the previous year. I was already comfortable in the college setting, and my grades gave me confidence to continue my hard work. My classes that semester were interesting and kept my mind active. After class, it was time to get back to work on the field.

It would be safe to say that my career as a football player was full of up and downs. It was comparable to an intense roller coaster at one of those amusement parks. With every up, came a down. With every down, came an up. The ups and downs happened so fast that there was no time to adjust. Starting my first game as a college football player was definitely an up; what followed next was definitely a down.

During one of our normal blocking drills in practice, something was different. When I released my block from the defender, I had an incredible amount of pain in my right thumb. I couldn't bend my thumb without getting nauseous. I went back in for the next play, but found even more pain. I knew I couldn't keep playing like that, but I didn't want to forfeit my starting role over a stupid injury. I came too far to be turned away that quickly.

After practice, I talked to the team's doctor about my thumb. Because of the pain, I assumed I broke it and wouldn't be able to play anymore. The doctor examined my thumb and told me he had both good news and bad news. The good was I didn't break my thumb and would eventually be able to play. The bad news was I sprained my thumb badly and he suggested that I take a couple of games off. I knew that wasn't even an option because any time on the bench gave someone else an opportunity to take my position. He did tell me, though, that as long as I kept my thumb taped up, I couldn't do any more damage to it. I would, however, be in a lot of pain.

He was right. I was able to keep my starting position during the second game. I took his advice and taped up my thumb. Even though it hurt every time I blocked someone, I was still able to block. I went the entire game in extreme pain, not letting anyone get by me. We ended up winning that game and I learned a valuable lesson; from then on, I always taped my fingers and thumbs before hitting the field.

The injury seemed to improve as the season went on. I continued to tape my fingers before every practice and every game. Though I wasn't playing at full capacity, it was better than not playing at all. I had really earned that spot on the starting line, and no one was going to take it from me. I knew that because I made it through that second game, I could make it through all of them. I wasn't ready to let a minor injury end my career.

Chapter 57

We considered it a successful season, even though we didn't go undefeated, after beating Faith Community College and coming close to a victory over Byron Junior College. Our record was good enough to make it to the Michigan Junior College Conference playoffs; a feat that we were unable to accomplish the previous season. As a playoff contender, we had the same chance of going to a post-season game that any other playoff team in our conference had. We had already achieved the goal our coach had set out for us a few months prior, and were two victories away from a post-season game.

More importantly, I personally had a successful season. As an offensive lineman, I started in almost every play that our offense ran, and not once did I let a defender get past me. When our running back ran towards my side of the offensive line, he always found a safe way through. I wasn't just part of an offensive line; I was the foundation of a successful starting line. My short term goal was to continue my success for three more games. By having a flawless season, there would be no way the University of Southern Michigan would overlook me.

Throughout the season, I was also able to maintain my good grades. During my first year of college, I was able to develop a way to balance practice, studying, and time in the weight room so that I could work on my classes while not taking time away from football. I needed to know that I had grades good enough to transfer, and definitely good enough to be a student-athlete at the University. I wanted to guarantee that my grades would not stand in the way of my dream.

Mike was also having a successful season. He broke his personal records from the previous season, and was making a name for himself as one of the best running backs in major college football. He averaged over 2 touchdowns a game and almost 200 yards of rushing. Without Mike, they would not have an 11-win season. Sadly, his grades didn't improve. He was staying above the required 2.0 average, but not by much. Clearly, he was more dedicated to football than to school. We never started out as good students, but it was still sad to see him abandon the study habits that we had finally developed in high school.

Chapter 58

Even though we weren't in the playoffs the previous season, I was still familiar with the playoff atmosphere. As predicted, the intensity rose at practice, and everybody took a more serious approach. The coaches were focused, and increased our daily huddles with lectures of encouragement. Unlike high school, we only had two games ahead of us. Although it didn't sound like a big challenge to win two games, we would be playing against teams that were as committed as we were.

We had made it in to the conference playoffs by only losing two games. One of those losses came from Whitaker Technical College. Whitaker Tech lost one more game than we did, which put them two spots below us in the conference standings - at 4th place. The 3rd place spot just below us belonged to Faith Community College. They ended their season with two losses as well, but one of those loses came from us, so it was their year to lose the tie-breaker. At the number one spot was Byron Junior College. They were used to the top spot in the playoffs as they had taken that position five seasons in a row. They finished the season undefeated. They were ranked number three in the nation, and needed to win the conference playoffs in order to have a chance at making it to the junior college title game.

Because of our identical records, we played Faith Community in the first round, while Byron played Whitaker Tech. In our win over Faith earlier in the season, we were able to discover a couple of weaknesses. We were able to take advantage of those weaknesses in our victory during that game and when we played them again in the playoffs, those weaknesses were still there. Once again, we leveraged their weaknesses and moved on to the second round of the playoffs.

During the game, I continued my pattern of not letting anyone get by me. Even though Byron was the third best junior college team in the nation, their big guys up front were no match for me. They gave me a fight, but I still won every time. I was getting the hang of playing football at the college level. Unfortunately, that was the only bright spot in the game for me. We quickly discovered why Byron Junior College was ranked so high nationally; they embarrassed us. They finished our season.

Mike had a different post-season run. With their one loss, USM wasn't ranked high enough to make it to the championship game. Southern Michigan did, however, make it to another New Year's Day game. That time, with Mike leading the way, they won their prestigious game, and ended up as the number two major college football team in the country.

Chapter 59

At the conclusion of the season, I was in limbo. I considered the season successful for our team because we made it to the playoffs. I would declare it an even more successful season for me personally as I went the entire season playing nearly every play and not letting anyone get past me. Optimistically, I checked in with the University of Southern Michigan recruiter. I learned that all I could do at that point was wait.

I spent two seasons under the impression that I would have to stick out at Whitaker Junior College for Southern Michigan to notice me. I thought that my only chance of getting in would be to impress them enough that they would have to give me a chance on their team. The recruiter explained to me the reality of transferring to a four-year school from a junior college. As it turned out, everybody had a chance to try out for the team. In the summer time, they would hold tryouts for any football player wanting to walk onto the team. Sadly, these "walk-ons" were never rewarded with free tuition. As a matter of fact, of the over 100 players on the team, only 85 of them would receive a scholarship. He also added that, of the over 100 walk-ons trying out, typically only five of them made it to the team.

After yelling at the recruiter about the last two years I just wasted the junior college level, he convinced me that my time wasn't a total waste. During our initial conversation, the plan was for me to play at the junior college level so that I could gain experience playing at the college football level. At the tryouts, I would have the huge advantage of experience as a college football player - something many of my competitors wouldn't have. I would understand the intensity and drive needed to make the cut. To my benefit, the coaches also took experience and game play into account when making their decisions. The recruiter concluded that my grades were well above the 2.0 needed to transfer and, based on my incredible season as a starter, as long as I survived the try-out process, I would have nothing to worry about.

Mike was discouraged at first to hear my news. He hadn't understood the process either as he didn't have to try out. As one of those 85 scholarship players, he had done enough on the high school field to impress the coaches. After hearing *all* of my conversation, however, he understood my optimism.

Mike was already getting ready for his junior year. While I was waiting patiently for try-outs to begin, he was taking part in the spring practices. After winning their post-season game, USM had raised their next goal to winning the national championship. They were one win away from getting there the previous season, and they wanted to make sure that their one defeat wouldn't happen again. At the same time, not only had he developed a giant target on his back due to his successful season, he also wore that target because he was a pre-season candidate for the Gilreath Honor Award.

At the end of every major college football season, the Gilreath Award was presented on national television to the best athlete in major college football as decided by a jury of former athletes. The trophy was named after Nathan Gilreath, a player from the 1960s. In the late 60s, Gilreath, one of the best major college football players of his day, was well on his way to the professional level. However, instead of going to the pros, he enlisted as a Marine and was sent to Vietnam. After a distinguished career in the military, he returned home a highly decorated National hero. The league decided to honor him and acknowledge his career in college football by naming a trophy after him. Each year, a major college football player was honored for their individual performance at the collegiate level, while honoring Nathan Gilreath's dedication and service to his country.

Chapter 60

My six months of patiently waiting was up. I was done with my sophomore year of college and ready for the next step in my career. I ended up with 60 credits from Whitaker Junior College, which was enough to transfer to any four-year program. I also ended up with a 3.8 grade point average. My parents were quite proud and took me out for a fancy dinner. Rather than enjoying the dinner as a celebration, I saw it as a transition. It marked the end of my junior college days, and the beginning of my major college days.

Weeks later, I took the long drive to the opposite end of the state. Although Mike wouldn't have to try out for the team, he was there to support me. The try-outs were held on the same practice field used by the football team. For the try-outs, we had the field to ourselves, which really made us feel like we were already a part of the team. When I arrived, Mike introduced me as his best friend from high school, as well as the best offensive tackle in the state of Michigan, to the lineman coach. As much as I liked the title, I wasn't crazy about the pressure it put on me.

Try-out week wasn't as bad as I thought it would be. In fact, I was very thankful for those two years at Whitaker Junior College because they definitely prepared me for the work load that week. The first day was spent generating basic statistics. The coaches wanted objective numbers that they could use to compare us. They measured our height, weight, time it took to run 40 yards, our maximum bench press, and the time it took us to run an obstacle course (which tested our agility and quick turning). I was measured at 6'1", and topped the scale at just over 300 pounds. Although my weight hadn't changed much since high school, most of my weight came from muscle rather than fat. I was able to bench press 350 pounds and I ran 40 yards in just over five seconds.

The second day, we were placed into groups based on what position we wanted to play. At USM, there was a coach for every position. That meant that my group consisted only of offensive linemen. It made it easier for the coaches to compare us, and it made it easier for me to assess my competition. Once in our groups, we ran drills that demonstrated, according to our offensive line coach, our mental and physical capabilities. Basically, they wanted to see how much we could handle physically, and where our mental breaking point was. Due to my experience, I could handle much more than most of the others, and the coaches never could find my breaking point.

At the end of the day, our measurements were posted. Mike told me they did that so we could compare ourselves to each other. For some players, they used the comparison as motivation to get faster, bigger, or stronger. For other players, they became intimidated by their competition and would end up quitting. The coaches enjoyed the latter because they didn't want guys on their team who became easily intimidated. Mike was impressed by my numbers. My weight was within range, but my height was about an inch short of what they wanted, which I couldn't do anything about. My bench press was above average, while my 40-yard time gave me the reputation of being the fastest for someone my size.

As the week progressed, the number of walk-ons started dwindling. By the last day, the initial number of participants was cut from 120 to 64. At the beginning of the day, the coaches brought everyone together and listed off 44 names. Those guys were in a group of players that "showed effort, but it wasn't enough". They were done. The remaining 20 guys were those who needed to be "reevaluated for further decision". I felt like I was on one of those reality singing shows and I had just made it to the final round. Although I wasn't quite on the team, my competition went from 119 to 19.

The coaches then wanted to get our basic stats again. They used the same methods that they had used in the beginning of the week, but for whatever reason, they wanted to record those numbers again. Impressively, my bench press went up by 10 pounds, while my 40-yard time was cut by a fraction of a second. I even gained a little more weight. Once the assessment was over, we were called back for one last meeting. The coach told us they had reassessed us to see if we were capable of progression in a short amount of time. He read a list of names at that time; mine wasn't on it. He then thanked those guys for showing up, but if they wanted to be on the team, they would have to demonstrate the ability to progress. To the rest of us, he said he would see us the following week on the practice field.

Chapter 61

Even though I had been on the campus for a week, I only had a chance to see the practice field during tryouts. We didn't have much time to do any sightseeing, and we slept on the floor of a complex next to the practice field. Understandably, they didn't want us to get too used to the luxuries of the campus setting, knowing that most of us wouldn't last the week of try-outs.

Mike knew that, so he was more than happy to take me on a tour of the campus. The practice field was right across from the football stadium. The coach wanted us to be able to see the stadium from the practice field to motivate us and remind us what we were trying out for. It was exciting to now be inside the stadium. The stadium was similar to the one at Northeastern, only this one was soon to be mine. I could accept that I wouldn't spend much time on the playing field, but I would at least be on the sidelines.

Next on our tour were the dorms. They were impressive. The dorms were still on the campus, but were in a separate area away from everything else. They were massive. Most of them were over six stories tall, and easily roomed a thousand students. The campus was pretty old, so the dorms weren't pretty. Most of the windows had air conditioners sticking out of the windows, and the exterior walls looked aged. One of the dorms stood out a little, though. That one looked brand new and didn't have any air conditioners in the windows. That was the one that Mike walked me through.

Once inside, I could feel the cold air circulating through the main lobby. The building was very clean and the walls were freshly painted. Even the staff at the counter were friendly and addressed us as "gentlemen." Mike told me that this was the athlete's dorm. The dorm was reserved for scholarship student-athletes. The college wanted to make sure the athletes were taken care of and were happy with their housing arrangements so that they wouldn't want to go to a more comfortable university. I, personally, didn't want to leave. Their plan worked.

I was even more impressed when Mike showed me his room. I'd known him for most of my life, so I knew the nice furniture, the big screen TV, the video game system, and the computer weren't really his. As it turned out, the school even furnished the rooms for the athletes to make sure they had all of the comforts and essentials necessary to stay focused on the game. The computer was meant for studying, the television for reviewing game footage, and the video game system could be used as a simulator to run various plays. His room was divided for two students.

In the athletic dorm, athletes were paired with other athletes of the same sport. They even had separate floors for different sports. Football players were on the top floor so that they could see the stadium from their rooms. I could see why; the view was breathtaking. Mike told me to get used to the view since I would be his new roommate.

Chapter 62

When we came back to the practice field the following Monday, the five of us on the practice squad were suddenly part of a large group again. We didn't know what was going on, and were concerned that we would have to tryout against those guys as well. Even though we were ready for it, we were relieved to discover that the big group was actually the rest of the team. Apparently, they were off the previous week due to the heat. Since they were already on the team, they didn't need to suffer during the hottest time of the year. The five of us were pulled to the side and explained our role.

Even though we were official Dragons, and just as much a part of the team as any of the other players, we had the important role of being on the scout team. The scout team consisted of 23 players; 11 on defense, 11 on offense, and one kicker. Each of us had our own position with no backup. The coaches figured that if we needed to take a break during practice, we didn't need to be on the team. It was our responsibility to learn the plays and formations of the teams that the Dragons would be playing against. During the practice week, we would emulate that team so that USM would know what they were up against at the end of the week. The following week, we would have to quickly learn the plays and formations of the next team. The coach then gave us the rest of the bad news. Even though we were given the difficult task of studying 12 different teams over the course of 12 weeks, without ever taking a break, the scout team was not allowed on the sidelines during the game, and would not travel with the team to away games.

On the scout team, there were two coaches. Mine was the offensive coach. His job was to make sure our offensive group memorized and emulated flawlessly the team we were scouting for each week. He told us that even though we were on the scout team, we should still be proud of ourselves for being part of the team as a whole. We had a very important role because we allowed our teammates to be better prepared for the week. More preparation meant a better chance of winning games. It was up to us to be flawless during practice because if we messed up, our team of starters could not practice efficiently. Rather than viewing ourselves as the scout team, it was suggested that we view ourselves as players from major college football teams from all over the country; a different player every week. If we still struggled with all of that, there were many others out there who were willing to take our place.

After being inspired by the coach, we were ready to be assigned our positions for what would be the rest of the season. It was easy to figure out who would take what positions on our offensive line. One of our guys was the center on the team that won the National Junior College Title Game the previous season. Two more were considered some of the best linemen in Michigan high school football, but weren't good enough to earn scholarships, and felt they were too good to play at the junior college level. One was a left guard, while the other was a left tackle. A fourth guy played right guard at Byron Junior College the previous season, which conveniently left me with the right tackle position. Our offensive line was made up of the best offensive linemen who couldn't make the USM depth chart, but could've easily started for any junior college. Although it would've been impossible for us to win any games at this college level, we made it our goal not to be losers.

Chapter 63

The scout team spent the rest of the summer training with the rest of the team. The summer practices were similar to the practices I endured at Whitaker Junior College. The entire team spent the summer together working on our speed and strength. Our scout team was full of athletes with various college playing experiences, so the coaches wanted to make sure that we were all at the same level. It was their goal to get us all to the same intensity so that we could compete with the starters. We spent long days under the hot sun running, blocking, and hitting with the rest of the team.

The weight room was nothing like I had ever seen before. The room itself was amazing. All of the machines were brand new, and the room included every piece of equipment imaginable. While in the weight room, the coach had a specific workout routine created for each of our position groups. The routine for the offensive linemen was more intense than any routine I had ever created for myself. The routine also came with a meal plan which allowed for healthy eating while rapidly increasing muscle growth. Those routines would make us stronger and leaner than ever before and would allow us to compete at the major college level.

As the summer went on, I could feel myself getting stronger. I had already gained 10 pounds of muscle, and added more weight to my bench press. I was even losing inches off of my waist. Although I was already on a high protein diet, it was the first time that I was actually watching what I was eating. Not only was I getting stronger, but I could also run faster and breathe easier.

Mike didn't change as much as I did over the summer. He had already been on the team for two seasons, so the coaches had plenty of time to mold him into the player they needed. As a candidate for the Gilreath Award, he had to work on his speed. The teams we would be playing against that season would make it their primary objective to stop him. They would have to catch him first, though.

Practices weren't fun by any means, but after two years, at least we were back on the same field again. As teammates, Mike and I were able to push each other, and keep each other focused on what needed to be done for the upcoming season. When we weren't practicing, we spent the summer in our air conditioned dorm room playing video games and surfing the internet. Not only were we hanging out together on a daily basis like we used to, but we were finally able to do it without worrying about breaking rules or getting into trouble. We were finally adults, able to make our own decisions.

A week before regular season practice was set to begin, we were given a week off. The coach wanted to reward us for a good summer practice, and wanted our bodies to be prepared for the upcoming season. Mike and I decided to go home that week. We drove in a car that we had bought together. The car that his parents bought for him had already died and since, thanks to my parents, I didn't have to pay for college, I was able to put some money towards a more reliable car. The car got us home safely where we spent a week with our families and old friends. I was able to visit my former junior college coach and brag about making the team. The week flew by as it was time to say goodbye to our families. We headed back to campus for four months of college football fun.

Chapter 64

We came back to practice the Monday following our break. The scout team was separated from the regular team. After spending the summer getting in shape with the rest of the team, we were given our own practice field where we could run our own practices. While on the field, our scout team coach explained to us the plan for the week ahead. During the first two days of practice, we would be working on scouting the team that the Dragons would be playing at the end of the week. The first day we would watch their game film and study what our individual roles would be. The coaches would use that time to look at the other team as a whole, and understand what plays they ran during specific situations. The second day, we would work on the selected plays in our small groups. The last two days, we would work with the rest of the team so they could see what plays the other team ran. First we would walk through those plays and how they aligned with our team's plays. Then, on that last day, we would run a scrimmage that would be similar to a dress rehearsal. In the scrimmage, both the starting offense and defense would play against the scout team. The team was given Friday off to recover; that day would also be used as a travel day for away games. On game days, the scout team would only be able to watch the games from the stands and only if we bought a ticket for the game. Our weight room time during game week would be spent with the rest of the team after practice, which allowed us to work out in our positional groups.

Just like the coach said, we went right into the team film room. Our scout team watched a game from last season involving the team we would be playing. Even though our schedule would start with four weaker teams outside of our conference, our coaches still took every game seriously. I watched their right offensive tackle the entire time during that first film. After the film room, we went to the weight room to work out with the rest of the team. The offensive linemen and I had already created a bond, so I found those guys fun to work out with and looked forward to that part of the day.

The following day, we worked again in our scout team. It was a pretty easy day for me as my job wasn't too challenging. But two days into the week, I was given an opportunity to finally block a real defender. As a lineman in junior college, no one got by me. I was only hoping I would have that kind of success for another season. My power and speed had grown rapidly over the summer, but I would still be blocking against a defender who was a starter for two New Year's Day post-season games.

After two unchallenged years, my success was finally halted. I think my nerves got the best of me because, when the ball was snapped, I froze. The giant defensive end got past me in record time. For the next play, I got my head back in the scrimmage; I had to if I wanted to stay on the team. I imagined the other guy was just another player in junior college. When I stood up, I was no longer intimidated. I did what came naturally and held the guy up at the line. For the rest of the day, he struggled against me. At the end of the scrimmage, I was confident in my job and knew I could handle football at this new level.

We again went back to the weight room at the end of practice. I was extremely motivated because I finally felt the results of the new workout routine with my new group. Those results told me that my hard work in the weight room was paying off, and as I worked harder, the outcome would be even better. Once we were done with our work out, the coach told the players on the team where and when to meet on game day. And just like that, the week was over for me. I had three days off to myself. I knew I should've been happy for the extended weekend, but instead I felt left out.

Chapter 65

I spent the entire weekend getting ready for the start of classes. I didn't know what the semester would bring, but I knew I would have to be prepared if I wanted to keep up my impressive grades. Classes hadn't started yet, so there wasn't any school work to study. Instead, I studied the campus and how to get to my classes from where I was. I also looked up my teachers online so that I had an idea of who would be teaching my classes. Finally, I made sure I had all of my supplies, clothes, essentials, etc.

During the game on Saturday, I watched the guys on our team. I knew most of them and I wanted them to do well. They were the people that I had worked hard with in practice and I knew they deserved success. I kept a good eye on the defensive end that I worked against in practice. Rather than viewing him as competition on the line, I was able to see him as a student and wanted him to use my lessons of getting past a tough offensive tackle. Every time he did, I felt better about myself as a teacher. I felt like all of my hard work at practice was paying off, not just for me, but for him as well.

A few days later, I was ready for my first class. It was held in the lecture hall I had expected two years ago. It was a room of nearly 300 students. The chalkboard was the size of a billboard, and the professor looked like anything you could imagine from TV. We never introduced ourselves, nor did we get a chance to say anything. He spent the entire two hours talking, and we spent the entire two hours taking notes.

The next class was nearly similar. The only difference was, in that class, I noticed her. She was perfect. Christine was the prettiest girl in the class, and she made me smile just looking at her. Her eyes seemed to speak to me. After class, she came over to me and told me she had been in my previous class. She could tell that I was keeping up with the professor. She apologized because she knew I was a football player and that, at first, she thought I was just another dumb jock. She suggested that we could hang out sometime during the week to exchange notes. We then exchanged numbers.

I nearly ran to the dorm to tell Mike about her. He told me that my symptoms were common for someone who was falling in love. I had never been that crazy about a girl before, so I didn't know what to do next. He told me he had been in love numerous times while at school, and would be able to give me great advice. He told me to treat the situation like I would a practice. Instead of worrying about the end result, I would have to do what I was used to doing and worry only about the task at hand. In that situation, what I was used to doing was being myself. The task at hand was simply exchanging notes without letting my feelings trip me up.

After seeing Christine the following day in yet our third class together, I knew it was meant to be. After practice that day, I called her up to study. She came over to our dorm because we had air conditioning that actually worked. After exchanging notes for an hour, we exchanged conversation. We didn't stop talking until the next morning. Mike teased me for not getting past first base, but I was just happy to be on the field.

Chapter 66

The next five weeks felt like they could not have gotten any better. I continued to become stronger, and no one got past me on the line. I could tell by our scrimmages that I was easily the most athletic lineman on the scout team's offensive line. The defender that I blocked against was also reaping the rewards because he already had the most tackles by a defensive linemen in our conference. He told me that after going against me in practice, the guys on the other teams were a cake walk. The team was doing great because, after six games, they hadn't lost yet. Mike was even doing great and remained the top candidate for the Gilreath Award. In those first five games, we were able to beat four non-conference teams, as well as one team in our conference. Because we hadn't lost in the conference, we were tied for first place. Our team was also ranked in the top-10 of all major college football teams. Finally, and most importantly, in those five weeks, I spent a lot of time with Christine. Some of that time was actually spent studying.

Midway through the sixth week of practice, those five weeks somehow got better. After a particularly intense lifting session, one of the linemen asked me if I wanted to go to the bar with him. I knew it was trouble because neither one of us were old enough to drink and probably wouldn't even be allowed in a bar. Even if we were old enough, players weren't allowed to party during the week. I backed out by telling him I had a big date with my girlfriend (which I actually did).

In the morning I was called into the football office by the team's offensive line coach. Apparently, I made the right choice the night before in not going out. The coach asked me about my teammate's offer to go to the bar. He wanted to know exactly what happened. I told him simply that the guy asked me to go to the bar with him and I told him no. The coach reinforced that drinking while on the team was forbidden by the school. Drinking underage, however, was forbidden by law and would have to be dealt with. The team took a serious zero-tolerance approach to minors drinking and, after being caught, they planned on kicking the player off the team. With him off the team, a spot was open on the offensive line. The coach told me that I wouldn't be rewarded for making the right decision because my decision to not drink was an expectation. However, I would be rewarded for my hard work during the season.

The coach told me that I was the best offensive lineman on the scout team. The guy who ended up getting kicked off the team was the team's backup center. They wanted me to fill the role, but knew I didn't have any experience as a center. The coach would understand if I didn't want to accept the offer because I didn't feel comfortable at that position. However, I knew I would be foolish for turning down any offer, even if it meant I had to be the kicker. Once I accepted the position, he explained his plan for me. It began with me taking the scholarship from the player that I replaced; I would be able to spend the rest of my time at college tuition-free.

After telling Mike about the great news, I called my parents to tell them what was going on. First, I made the news official that I had a girlfriend. They knew I was dating someone, but I never gave them too much information until that conversation. Next, I told them about my opportunity on the team. I told them to be sure to watch the game on TV and look for me; but instead of watching from home, they wanted to come and see the game in person. Lastly, I told them that they wouldn't have to worry about my college expenses anymore. My parents were by no means wealthy, so paying for two years of my schooling would've eventually been a struggle for them. They were stunned that I was now one of the 85 students receiving free education, compliments of the USM football team.

The rest of the week I spent practicing as a center. The job of a center was pretty easy; I simply snapped the ball when instructed, and then blocked the defender in front of me. The actual snapping part was the challenge. In practice, rather than working out in our small groups during the first two days of practice, I spent the long days working strictly on my snaps. During the two scrimmage days, the coach gave me a little extra time on the field to try my new position against real defenders. At the end of the week, rather than going back to the dorm for a three day weekend, I was able to meet with the team on Saturday. I had finally made it to game day!

Chapter 67

My first game playing for the team was a nationally televised game. The game would be a night game and would be broadcasted across the country. That meant that someone in Oregon would be able to turn on their TV and watch our game. Even though our game was scheduled to kick off at 8PM, our team met in the dorm lobby at 3PM. From there, we walked as a team to the University Center. There, we ate a big meal as a team. Afterwards, we discussed the game plan and how to successfully defeat our opponent. The atmosphere was exciting, yet serious. Just like with any pre-game day, the team was on a mission and it was time to work.

From the University Center, we walked in unison to the stadium two hours prior to kickoff. The hard part was maintaining my 'game face'. As we walked to the stadium, we were led by a police escort and surrounded by fans and television cameras. On the way to the stadium, we walked past a bronze statue of a dragon placed in the middle of campus. Our school's marching band was there and played the fight song as we came into sight. As we walked past the dragon, each team member had to slap the dragon for luck; a tradition that had lasted for over 50 years.

When we finally made it to our locker room, our game day uniforms were waiting for us. I was stunned when I saw my last name on the back of a black and red jersey hanging from a locker, which also had my name across it. Once the shock wore off, I put my uniform on. Mike's locker was next to mine and, as we realized the next chapter of our dream was about to be fulfilled, we couldn't stop grinning.

Once dressed, the team walked onto the indoor field for a few practice drills and then went back into the locker room for a pre-game speech. With only 10 minutes to go before kickoff, we made our way back to the field. That time, we stopped at the entrance of the tunnel. The stadium went dark. I could make out something large being dragged in front of the tunnel. I knew this was the giant head of a black dragon with bright red eyes. I remembered watching the dragon emit a ball of fire in Wyoming the previous year, and it gave me chills. Now, the chills had returned, only this time I was the one running through the dragon's smoky mouth.

I spent the rest of the game on the sidelines as the backup center. Just like in junior college, backup offensive linemen were not often used. The starters stayed in the entire game and only sat if they were injured. If they were too tired to play an entire game, they wouldn't be able to play an entire season. Even as I watched the game from the sidelines, I knew it was much better than watching another game from home.

We finished the day with six wins for the season; Mike finished with 4 touchdowns and nearly 300 yards. Even though he still had the target on his back, other teams still hadn't found a way to slow him down. Without me on the scout team, the defender who practiced against me was still able to remain ahead of the other defensive linemen in the conference with the most tackles. I was suddenly a big part of a team that was halfway through their season, and hopefully a true candidate to play in the Major College Football Championship Game.

Chapter 68

The second half of the season was similar to the first half. While winning the rest of our six remaining games, Mike continued to be a statistical phenomenon, while our defense continued to dominate. I kept practicing my snaps as a center and watched the games from the sidelines, waiting patiently for my chance to play. During my down time, Christine and I continued to study and remained top students. As a couple, we pushed ourselves to maintain good grades and even turned it into a competition.

At the end of the season, we were ranked as the second best team in the country. We remained undefeated, and were projected to make it into the national championship game. A few days later, it was officially announced that the Major College Football Committee would match us up against Alaska State University in the Major College Football Championship Game. No one saw it coming, but the Killer Whales went the entire season undefeated as well, and were actually ranked higher than us. It was believed that they had a higher rank because they faced stronger opponents in the Pacific Northwest Conference than we did in the Midwestern Conference.

Our team had five weeks to get ready for the game. We already knew who our opponent was, so we were able to spend the entire five weeks preparing for one team. We were working on the plays we were going to run, while training for the plays that we expected them to run. We spent some time on strength and conditioning, but most of our time was spent on the strategic part of the game rather than the physical part. A few weeks into practice, we took a break. We all had to stop and watch a trophy presentation.

A few days before the presentation, Mike was told that, as a candidate, he could bring one guest with him to the Nathan Gilreath Honor Award ceremony. Without hesitation, Mike told them he was bringing me. The day before the ceremony, they flew us to Dallas, Texas. We've seen big cities while traveling to games throughout the conference, but none of those cities were as big as the one we were at; it was the size of nearly 50 Whitakers put together. We were put up in a luxury room in a fancy hotel, given full access to room service, and treated to gourmet meals.

The following day, while I was exploring Dallas, Mike was being interviewed by all the major sports programs. Later that evening, we were all escorted to the Heartford Theatre. The theatre held nearly 2,000 people. Of those 2,000, only five of them were candidates. Other than the candidates and their guests, the rest of the audience paid big money to be at the ceremony. Two of those attendees were his parents. The tickets were costly, and the drive out was time consuming, but it was all worth it to personally witness as Michael Upton was chosen by the Major College Football Committee as the best college football player of the season.

Chapter 69

The target on his back went from big to huge. He was no longer a Gilreath *candidate*; he was a Gilreath *winner*. Rather than being *one of* the best major college football players, he was voted as *the* best major college football player. But even with the bigger target, the game plan didn't change.

A few days after the New Year's Day games were played, the Major College Football Championship Game was the only game left to play in the college football season. Only two teams remained: the University of Southern Michigan, and Alaska State University. Once the game was over, one team would be declared the best team in college football. With five weeks of practice behind us, we were ready to be that team.

The USM team was flown out to Little Rock, Arkansas a few days before game day. During those days, we were given time to explore the city and take part in media interviews. The media asked many different questions to many different players, but the common theme of their questions was what we were doing both individually, and as a team, to win the game. Prior to the interviews, we were instructed not to give away any strategy. With that in mind, the vague and generic answers provided by our players and coaches became, at some times, comical.

Soon, it was game day and fun time was replaced by game time. We had some serious games during that season, but this game meant the most. Luckily, the coach had been through of this type of atmosphere, so he had been preparing us all season by treating every game like a title game. That way, when the real title game finally arrived, we were ready for it. We knew our experience in the national spotlight would be a psychological advantage for us as Alaska had never been to a game like that one before.

The pre-game ritual remained intact as we made our way onto the field through the dragon's mouth. The one thing we weren't expecting was all the cameras. There were cameras everywhere. There was even a camera hovering over the field operated by a remote control. This game would be watched by nearly every person in all 50 states, and even those living in the American Territories. It was commonly known that pairing the two best teams in college football would lead to the best game of the season. They were right.

Chapter 70

Alaska was the strongest team we had faced all season. As much as they prepared to defend against Mike, he was still too fast for them and helped us out for most of the game. It wasn't a blowout, though, as their offense continued to match our touchdowns with touchdowns of their own. Towards the end of the game, we were trailing for the first time in the season.

With time running down, we were able to move the ball five yards shy of the end zone. We only had three attempts at scoring. We were down by six, so we had to score a touchdown to win the game. After two failed attempts with Mike trying to run the ball up the middle, we had to try something new. They were used to him now and figured out how to stop him from crossing the scrimmage line. Our coach used his last time out.

In the huddle, he called over the entire team. He looked right at me and asked me if I remembered playing in high stress football games in high school. I did. The coach then asked Mike the same thing. The coach told us that while watching tapes of our high school games while trying to recruit Mike, he noticed that East Whitaker performed their best during high stress situations by trying something that most teams wouldn't even think about doing. In those situations, our high school coach needed trustworthy players that he could depend on to fill key roles. Because Mike and I were able to prove ourselves in those situations, our coach felt that he could do the same.

The coach's plan put Mike at wide receiver and placed me as a running back. He brought up our state championship victory and how we won that game by using Mike as a wide receiver. The coach also brought up the game where I scored the game-winning touchdown against West Whitaker to give our team an undefeated season. Once we went back onto the field, the coach would be able to call a play based on how their defense reacted to our new offensive lineup.

As we ran out to our new formation, their defense panicked. Just like in the state finals, Alaska sent numerous guys over to cover Mike. Apparently, they also watched our high school championship game and knew what he could do as a receiver. With him triple-teamed, I would be the coach's best option. Once the ball was snapped, I secured it tightly in my belly. The last time I tried running the ball, I wasn't sure if I had scored or not. That night, there was no denying it. Once I crossed the line of scrimmage, I continued running until I jumped the six foot barrier and landed in the Dragon's student section.

Once the team was done celebrating on the field, it was time for the country to celebrate with us. A large stage was brought out to the middle of the arena where our coach was presented with the Major College Football National Championship Trophy. Next, one of our players was called up to the stage. That player would receive the Player of the Game Award. The award went to the player that made the biggest difference to the team during the title game. The award went to Mike. Not only was he now the best major college football player, having won the Gilreath Honor Award, but he was also part of the best major college football team, and recognized as the most valuable player during the championship game.

The next day, I was presented with an award of my own. It was an award that didn't get publicized much and, thus, was one that I had never heard of. At the conclusion of each major college football season, an award was given to the best major college football player who started that season as a walk-on player. Prior to scoring the national championship game-winning touchdown, I began my career as a walk-on player. My success may not have been recognized by the media, but at least one committee realized the impressive turn-around I had, as I was presented with the Jerome Vierling Award.

Chapter 71

In the week that followed the National Championship Game, Mike and I began collecting newspaper and magazine articles that talked about the game. We cut out any articles or pictures of us and hung them on the walls of our dorm room. Most of the articles discussed the entire game, but sometimes they focused on his performance or my game-winning touchdown. There were numerous pictures of me in the stands with the student section. I looked like I was having a great time because, of course, I was. That was the day I got my 15 minutes of fame.

With the new season starting soon, we had little time off to ourselves. My plan was to simply enjoy the time off until spring practice started in March. Mike had different plans, however. When I returned from class one day with Christine, he needed to talk. He knew I would end up sharing with her anyway, so he didn't mind if she stayed to listen. He told me that his grades were getting worse. We had just started the second semester of our junior year and he was already in academic trouble. If he stayed in school, he was sure he would be kicked out and would not be able to play his senior year. And that would, of course, jeopardize our chances of playing in the pros together. His solution was to declare himself eligible early for the pros.

Although it didn't happen often, only juniors in college could leave early to go to the pros. Just because they declared themselves, though, they weren't guaranteed a spot on a professional football team. And once he declared, he would no longer be eligible to play for USM. For him to declare, he would have to be confident that his talent was good enough for the professional level, otherwise he wouldn't be able to play football again. Unfortunately, his grades didn't leave him much of a choice.

While I enjoyed my time off in February, Mike was using that time to impress the professional scouts. During the month, the scouts invited potential candidates to attend an event that assessed the athletes based on numerous activities. The format was very similar to the try-out format at Southern Michigan. At the end of the week, athletes were compared to other athletes at their position, and were given a numerical grade based on those comparisons. That information would be used later by professional football teams, as they analyzed players they may consider for their team.

In March, as I was getting ready for spring practices, the scouts came to our campus. It was a chance for our athletes trying out for the pros to show off. During that time, the athletes would use the assistance of their coaches, and possibly other players, to show the scouts whatever they thought would impress them. That was their last chance to improve their odds of being considered by professional football teams.

In April, as I was participating in our annual spring scrimmage, he was with the other top athletes at the Selection Showcase, waiting to see if he made it. During Selection Showcase Week, all of the general managers representing professional football teams would gather together during a televised event and would take turns picking which college football players they wanted on their teams. Each team received one pick per round, in a seven-round format. Selection order was based on the team's performance during the previous season. The worst team got the first pick, while the best team got the last. As it turned out, our Michigan Knights had the worst record the previous season, winning only one game, so they were rewarded with the first pick. After a few minutes of the country wondering which college football player would be picked first, Michigan chose a running back. Suddenly Mike was not only the best running back in major college football that season, but also the first college football player picked that year to play at the professional level.

As they announced his name, he came on stage and stood with the team's general manager. The general manager was the one who made all of the important decisions for the Michigan Knights. Having made his best decision ever, they were now both facing a crowd of nearly 200 athletes, also waiting to be called, and twice as many reporters. Mike was handed a team hat and jersey to wear while pictures were taken of him shaking the hand of the general manager. Because Mike was the first player picked during the Selection Showcase, he was guaranteed to be the highest paid rookie that next season.

Chapter 72

As Mike was becoming a millionaire, I was getting ready for my final season of college football. I knew I wouldn't be one of the first ones picked during my Selection Showcase Week, but I also knew that I wouldn't be picked at all if I didn't have an impressive season. Much of that success would be contingent upon becoming a starter on an elite team. Luckily, the center that I backed up the previous season would no longer be on the team as he was graduating at the end of the school year. In fact, he was one of 14 starters not coming back after winning the title.

In our title run the previous season, 11 seniors were marking their fourth season of playing at USM together. During their sophomore year, those 11 athletes were all starting and had made it to a New Year's Day game. After losing that game, they blamed their loss on inexperience. The following year, that same group would be returning with a year of experience playing at the major college level. The additional experience attributed to their victory the following New Year's Day. During their senior year, that group would return for yet a third season together as starters, that time adding a running back who would end up being voted as the best football player in the country. Even though he made a big difference in the game, the national championship was in large part due to the three years of experience by the group of 11 starters who were able to form a strong team bond over their four seasons playing together. Unfortunately, with them graduating, and an additional three juniors declaring for the pros, our team was left with only eight experienced starters from our national championship team.

On one hand, our team was inexperienced, which dropped our pre-season rank to the lower half of the top-25 major college football teams. On the other hand, our coach would need players with experience to step up and fill the numerous vacant spots. Even though we may have had an inexperienced team, I had a great chance to step up and prove myself. The bonus was, as a returning championship team, most of our games would be televised around the country as more fans would be interested in our team. That meant my performance, if selected as a starter, would be witnessed by people outside of our conference, including scouts and general managers from professional teams.

At the spring scrimmage game, I got my first chance at starting. Because of my experience, I was placed on the first-string offense. The coach informed me that just because I was starting on the scrimmage team, didn't mean I would be a guaranteed starter and I would have to use the summer to earn my spot. During the spring game, I continued my streak of not letting anyone by me. The guard next to me had a similar record. He was the guard that played at Byron Junior College while I was at Whitaker. He would later become my new roommate.

While the walk-ons were trying out, I took advantage of the one week break by going home. Because Mike would be making enough money in the pros to buy whatever car he wanted, he let me keep the car that we had purchased together. Terence, my new roommate, had nowhere else to go, so he ended up going back home with me. The long car ride to Whitaker flew by as we were able to talk about football for most of the time. When we weren't talking, we were jamming out our new favorite band 'Mike Mains and the Branches'. When we arrived home, my parents were excited to meet a player from a national championship team. As the week went on, the excitement began to dissolve as they saw how much food Terence and I went through. When it was time to leave, my dad's wallet was able to breathe a sigh of relief.

Chapter 73

When we returned to campus, we got right back into summer practices. Those practices had a different feel as a player on the regular roster than it did as a player on the scout team the previous season. Even with a different feel, though, the practices were still something I was very comfortable with. During those practices, I continued to become stronger and faster. When I wasn't practicing, I was studying for summer school or spending time with Christine on an almost daily basis. Finally, after a long and hot summer, it was time to get ready for my final season as a college football player.

The first week of regular-season practice was completely different than it had been the previous season. Just like with the scout team, the regular team didn't waste any time at practice. Rather than spending the first two days studying the opponent, my new team used that time to hit hard and hit often. As a starting center, I got a lot of practice time to work on my snaps, standing up as soon as I snapped the ball and blocking hard the person standing in front of me.

At our practices, the coaches wanted more intensity out of us. They wanted us to be the biggest and fastest team in college football. Anytime we slowed down, our opponent could gain an advantage. Not only were we expected to work fast, there was also no concern for injury during practice. The only one who couldn't get hit during practice was the quarterback. Even though our offensive line was doing a great job at blocking for him, the quarterback was still protected by wearing a red jersey indicating that he couldn't be touched. Everyone else, however, was expendable. If a player was injured during practice, there were other players ready to take his place. That meant that the defender coming at me wasn't allowed to slow down at any point and wouldn't worry about injuring me. The fear of death made me that much quicker with my snaps.

After using the first two days to work on lots of plays and lots of hitting, the next two days were spent scrimmaging against the scout team. We walked through our plays on the third day, while the fourth day of practice was a full blown scrimmage. Scrimmage for me felt the same as a starter, compared to my time on the scout team. The speed, intensity, and hitting were identical in both situations. The only difference was that even though the scrimmage felt like a real game, our team of starters always won.

By the end of the week, taking a day off made more sense. While on the scout team, we spent the first three days going at a slow pace with an intense weight room session afterwards. The scrimmage on the fourth day was intense, but that only lasted a few hours. As a backup, the first two days were intense, but the second two were almost relaxing as I stood on the sidelines for more than half of the scrimmage and watched the starters. During my senior year, however, all four days were intense, and there was no way my body would've been able to handle a full game without some time off. During that day off, most of us never left our dorm rooms and rarely got out of our beds. Fortunately, I didn't have any Friday classes scheduled during the upcoming school year.

Chapter 74

On my last play as a major college football player the previous season, I scored a game winning touchdown in the Major College Championship Game. I knew, though, that most of my plays that followed that game wouldn't have the same outcome. In fact, all of the plays during the first game of my senior season were all pretty similar in that I snapped the ball perfectly, I stood up quickly, and I stopped the defender from getting in the way of our offense. After winning that first game, our team of young starters had the confidence needed to push on through the rest of the games that season.

We took that confidence and won the next three games. After four weeks, we had won all four non-conference games and were getting ready for the Midwestern Conference schedule to begin. In major college football, a team was guaranteed to play in the post-season as long as they had more wins than they had losses. In a 12 game season, we only needed three more wins that season to make it to the post-season.

In that four-week time span, my relationship with Christine continued to get more serious and we rarely spent time apart. Both of our grade point averages remained high. We were both closing in on a 3.9 average, and were still making a competition out of it. Unfortunately, Mike wasn't having a very successful first couple of weeks in the pros.

Even though the Knights had only won one game the previous season, they still decided to stick with their same game plan. They were known as a pass-heavy team and passed the ball twice as much as they ran. They weren't ready to use Mike as an all-star because they wanted him to adjust to life as a professional football player. He had the desired speed, but at the professional level, defenders were still able to catch him. They wanted him to work on not getting tackled once he got caught. That meant he had to spend more time in the weight room and less time on the practice field. He was still their starting running back, he just wasn't getting the ball as often as he had been in college.

Once we started into our conference games, our team hit the wall. We were only able to add two more victories to our overall record. With six wins for the season, we were one game short of going to the post-season. For the first time in three seasons, the University of Southern Michigan football team ended their year early, and wouldn't make it into the rankings of the top-25 major college football teams in the league.

As we were going through our slump, Mike was hitting his stride. The team started balancing out their play selection once they could depend on him more. Not only was he fast, but he was finally a challenge to take down. With more chances at carrying the ball, his stats increased exponentially. As he got the ball more, the team got better. They didn't make it to the playoffs, nor did he receive any awards, but they did tell him that because of his performance in the second half of the season, he would get the ball more often the following season.

Chapter 75

Of course our team was disappointed in the outcome of our season. I was, however, able to make the most of it. During my time as a starting center, I stopped the defender every time I was given the chance; a feat that was nearly impossible to accomplish by most offensive linemen at any level. I knew that my success during my senior year would increase my chances of becoming a professional football player. To cap off my successful season, I was selected as the best center in the Midwestern Conference. I was also selected as a top-5 center, competing against every center in Major College Football.

Fall semester drew to a close and, surprisingly, I was able to maintain my 3.9 grade point average. With only one semester of school left, I was almost done with studying, homework, and quizzes. I knew that even if I didn't turn in another paper, or test, during my spring semester, my grade point average would still be high enough for me to graduate. Even though I was proud of Christine for achieving the same grade as me, she was even more proud of me because I was able to do it while concentrating on football. She wasn't the only one who noticed, though.

At the end of the fall semester, Midwestern Conference officials gathered together to discuss who the best male and female student-athletes were. They only took two factors into consideration: grades, and athletic performance. The two athletes were rewarded for achieving highest academic honors, while contributing the most to their teams. My awards as a lineman displayed my contribution to the team, while my grades were high enough for me to be declared the most successful male student-athlete in the Midwestern Conference during the fall semester.

Chapter 76

As my awards and honors were piling up, my chances of getting selected by a professional football team in April were increasing. In February, I went to the same try-out that Mike attended the previous season. As a center, I was compared to other offensive linemen from around the country. My numbers had improved significantly from my try-outs with USM a few years before, but they were only average compared to the rest of the group. While trying out for USM, I was competing against athletes who weren't talented enough to earn a scholarship. While trying out for the pros, however, I was competing against the best linemen from the best college football teams.

Once March came around, I got another chance to show off my skills to the professional recruiters. When they visited our school, I was able to go over game tapes with them and show them what I could bring to their team. I then showed them how strong I was in the weight room. Finally, I showed them how talented I was by snapping the ball perfectly to a quarterback, who was positioned 20 yards away from me.

Selection Showcase Week had finally arrived. I watched the program from my house because I wasn't quite good enough to be flown out to the show like Mike had been. I watched anxiously with my parents, my girlfriend, and my offensive line coach, who were all there to support me. The event lasted three days. The first day was dedicated to the first two rounds, the second day was the second two rounds, and the last day would be the last three rounds of the draft.

The first day seemed to take forever as each team slowly made their first pick. The Knights didn't pick until halfway through the first round because they ended the previous season with a better record than half of the teams in the league. After not being picked by any of those teams, I was anxiously waiting for the Knights' decision. They desperately needed a talented lineman because they wanted to run the ball more often. They got their lineman but, sadly, it wasn't me. I went the rest of the day not being picked.

As the second day arrived, I figured I had a better chance of being picked because five linemen had already filled slots. The second day went a little faster, but my anxiety continued to increase. During the Knights' two picks that day, my anxiety turned into disappointment; and for a second day, they weren't the only team that didn't have a use for me.

By the third day, my last and only chance at being selected by a professional football team had come. The three rounds that day would give me an additional chance to be picked. After the first six rounds, I was the last lineman still available from the group of athletes selected by the Major College Football Committee. That made me the best available lineman from the major college level. All I needed was for one team to have a need on the offensive line. By the end of the day, not another lineman was selected.

I tried to get some clarity from my offensive line coach. He told me that I had nothing to be disappointed about because I earned every award I received. I worked hard, and played a key role in the success of our team. He then gave me an answer that I was already familiar with; my success was too late. The reason I wasn't recruited by any major colleges after high school was that my success only came towards the end of my season. If my entire high school career was as successful as my senior year playoff run was, I would've been a scholarship athlete for all four years of college. The line coach said something along the same lines. Even though I had more accolades than an Olympic swimmer, I only received them during one season. All of the linemen that went ahead of me during the Selection Showcase had the same awards I had, but had earned them over the course of multiple seasons.

Chapter 77

Even though my life as a football player was over, my life outside of football still went on. Christine and I both maintained our good grades, and both graduated with bachelor's degrees from the University of Southern Michigan. Her degree was in education, while mine was in business. Our joke was that we would be able to start our own teaching business after college.

As much as it was a joke, we really did have to think about life outside of college. Once college was over, what would we do? My parents were in northern Michigan, while hers were in Indiana. Without school, we lost the only place that we could call ours. Clearly, going back to our own families was not an option. Our relationship had gotten very serious and there would be no splitting us up. The only question was where did we want to go? We were both family types. Neither of us wanted to be far from our families, so neither one of us wanted to move to the other's home town.

Our decision was to move to a city that was reasonably between her hometown and mine. That, coincidently, put us about 30 minutes away from where Mike lived, just outside of Lansing. I felt that if we were to live together, we would be taking a very serious step in our relationship. I wanted to make sure that we were serious about each other. I couldn't think of a better way to find that out then to ask for her hand in marriage. After her parents gave me their blessing, I proposed on the first day of living in our new place. She said yes.

Mike came in for a small engagement party. After much celebration, he wanted to talk about football. He told me that even though I didn't get selected by a pro team during the Selection Showcase, my football life could still exist. If I was still serious about our goal, I would have to again work hard to achieve it, and would have to get to the next level in another non-traditional way. Just like at USM, the Knights also held try-outs for walk-on players. Unlike college, the walk-ons were allowed to participate in spring training with the rest of the team. After a long process, most of the walk-ons would be cut. Even if a walk-on was able to survive the exhausting process, they usually only made it as far as the practice squad; used to help the real team prepare for upcoming games. However, on a rare occasion, a member of the practice squad would be called up to be a part of the regular roster. Even though my best shot would only land me on the practice squad, I was willing to make the commitment. But as a man about to be married, my decisions weren't made on my own anymore. Christine and I were suddenly presented with our first major decision as a couple.

She knew how badly I wanted to play professional football, especially with Mike. She also knew how much I would regret it if I chose to cut my career short after a difficult six years of creating my own path. Our biggest obstacle was money. We were living together and had to pay rent. As recent graduates, we didn't have much money. Even if I made the practice squad, I wouldn't make nearly the kind of money that Mike was making. Additionally, I would only be paid during the football season and wouldn't make any money during the off-season.

Christine's solution was to use the money that I put into savings during college to pay rent while she found a job. Once she found a job that paid enough money, she would be willing to pay our rent, and other bills, while I chased my dream. If I didn't make the team, I would need to find a real job. If, however, I did make the team, I would be making enough money to help with the bills. During the off-season, I would have to use my degree to find a job outside of football which would help support to our new family.

Once a plan was agreed upon, Mike made a suggestion of his own. He enjoyed my commitment to play in the pros. He also enjoyed the support Christine had shown in making sure I got there. Once he knew that we were in this together, he decided to include her in our team. As a member of our team, he decided that he would invest in my dream. As a new millionaire, he spent his money foolishly on expensive cars and a large home. The building was so big that it could've easily been divided into two houses. He offered to move the two of us into his place so we wouldn't have to pay rent at all. And just like that, I was ready for the next stage in my life.

The Professional Years

Chapter 78

While waiting for us to move in with him, Mike was getting his house ready for us. Although his house was big enough for the three of us, he wanted to make sure that we had our own privacy. To do that, he built an addition to his house that would give us twice the living space we had in our apartment. As a gift, he also custom-tailored his home-gym to accommodate my personal workout routine that I adopted from the University of Southern Michigan.

I spent the entire month of June preparing for the new challenge ahead of me. I assumed that professional football would be more intense than college football, so I knew that I would have to keep up with my conditioning and strength on my own time That was easy to do while living with Mike. His gym was spectacular.

With my own personal equipment, and the workout routine that had helped increase my strength in college, I worked out nearly every day. When I wasn't in the gym, I was spending time with Christine making plans for our wedding the following summer. A summer wedding was an easy choice for us because we knew, if things went well, we would both have the summer off. She had already accepted a teaching job at a local elementary school.

The evenings were also fun in our new shared housing arrangement. Some nights I spent with just Christine, while other nights I spent with Mike and his teammates. His idea was for me to meet some of the guys on the team, and for them to know what kind of a hard worker I was. He wanted me to hear their stories so that I knew both the incentives of playing professional football, as well as the dedication and hard work it took. It was a great plan, however, I couldn't get over the fact that I was hanging out with celebrities. Mike was too young to hang out with the legendary veterans, but the young guys at our house were still heroes to me. They were the guys who I watched play football every Sunday afternoon. They were also the guys who made our driveway look like a foreign car dealership.

One afternoon, while hanging with my soon-to-be teammates, they started talking about the process of training camp. Apparently, it was something that everyone planning to make the team had to endure, even those who were on the team the previous season. Training camp was a two-week process used to evaluate the young players, while giving the veterans a chance to get back into shape. After those two weeks, teams played in four exhibition games used to give anyone surviving training camp a chance at playing professional football. Those games would be played at real stadiums, against real teams, but only the new guys would get most of the playing time. After the exhibition games, the team's roster would be cut down from 90 players to 75. A few days later, they would have to cut another 22 players. Of those not making the 53-man roster, eight were offered a job on the practice squad.

Chapter 79

Even though the training camp officially began on Monday, Mike and I drove to camp on Sunday for the team's mandatory orientation meeting. On the way there, Mike reminded me that he had gone through the same process a year ago. He also pointed out that he, as well as the other guys I had met, would be going through the same thing with me. Even though most teams had their rosters set prior to camp, everyone on the team had to go through the same drills, meetings, and practices at the same intensity level. That meant I was faced with the challenge of standing out amongst an elite group of football players, while trying to earn a spot on the team. We both agreed that, as a walk-on, I shouldn't be disappointed if my goal was only to make the practice squad; even doing that would be an amazing honor. After Mike calmed me down a little bit, I spent the rest of the car ride introducing him to the songs of Mike Mains and the Branches.

At the training field, I was briefly introduced to the offensive line coach. Mike told the coach about my awards and hard work, both on and off the field. The previous season was only Mike's first season on the team, but as the starting running back, all of the coaches listened to what he had to say. His words wouldn't get me a spot on the team, but they would definitely put me in the spotlight. With the added attention, it was up to me not to let Mike down while showing the coaches that I could be one of their best linemen.

The veterans on the team already knew what was going on, but the coach still explained the schedule to the rest of the group. Our days would start out early with a team breakfast, followed by an hour of lifting. From there, we would have an hour long team meeting. That meeting would be followed by another hour of reviewing video of previous practices in our positional groups. At 10AM, we would go through a two hour walk-through practice in which we didn't use pads. After lunch, we would take part in another two hour practice, that time going full-contact. After that practice, we would have more meetings, followed by a 10PM curfew.

With the schedule laid out, we were given the rest of the day to get used to our new quarters. The training camp was held at a local college where we would be sleeping in dorm rooms. Again, Mike and I were roommates. While in our room, I started telling Mike my plan for training camp. I told him that I wasn't worried about waking up early, or learning new plays at the meetings. I was great at memorizing plays and knew I wouldn't have to memorize that much as a center. My biggest target would be the two hour practice after lunch. While others would fear it, I would have to look forward to it. It would be my only chance to fight for a spot on the practice squad. During those two hours, I would have to block my strongest, hit my hardest, and run my fastest just to keep up with the rest of the team.

Chapter 80

By 7AM the next morning, we were all in line waiting for a hearty cafeteria breakfast. Then, after a lifting session, we met as a team and talked about the basic game plans of the Michigan Knights. That meeting led into the next meeting just for offensive linemen. There, we talked about the offensive line from the previous season. Those five linemen stood up and introduced themselves. The line coach said that they would be the starters during the upcoming season, while the rest of us would have to fight each other for backup roles. With 10 of us left, we knew that five of us would be sent home, as there were only five backup positions left on the roster. Some were upset by that news because they thought that being picked during Selection Showcase Week guaranteed them a spot on the roster.

While the other guys went to the locker room to get their helmets, I was held up by the offensive line coach. He told me that Mike was the only reason why I was given a shot to make the team. At that point, it would be up to me to make it to the end of training camp on my own. He acknowledged that I was one of the best linemen in college football, but told me that the professional level was full of the *best* football players from some of the *best* football teams across the country. The guys in the room with me were no bigger than I was, but the coach assured me that they had a lot more experience than I did.

Instead of breaking me down, the coach ended up inspiring me. He was right; I was on my own and I would only have myself to blame if I went home. I had the exact same chance to earn a spot on the team as those picked during the Selection Showcase. I took that inspiration with me out to the practice field. I didn't allow myself to be overwhelmed by the fact that I was on the same field as football legends; hanging out with Mike's friends helped me get past that feeling. Instead, I paid attention to what the coaches were saying the entire time and succeeded in not stopping practices so that the coaches could yell at me.

After a light lunch, I was ready to block. Even though it was only the first day of practice, nobody held back. We only had 10 days to show what we were made of, and nobody was going to waste that time. I continued working with the offensive linemen in our blocking and running drills. Halfway into that practice, we got our first chance at live contact. Similar to my first practice in college football, the first hit was the hardest. As I stared up into the sky, the only thing I could think of was that I had just been run over by a semi-truck driven by one of my favorite defensive linemen. While some people paid to get his autograph, I was one of the lucky ones who had his cleat tattooed on my stomach.

Practice continued to be painful. Even though I continued to get run over, I bounced back up every time. I knew that I wasn't quite ready to play at the professional level, but I sure wasn't going to let people think I was a quitter. The team's doctor even made me feel at ease. He told me that he normally saw about 20 players after the first day of training camp. *Most* of those made it back the second day.

Finally, after dinner, I could say that I survived my first day of professional football training camp. I was bruised, tired, bloody, and couldn't raise my hands over my head, but I was excited that I would have a chance to do it all over again the following day. Back in the room, Mike wanted to make sure I wasn't too discouraged. He knew that I had been working my butt off in the off-season, and didn't want me to get discouraged because I was literally being walked all over. He told me that even the strongest players looked like they had just finished 10 rounds with the champ after their first day of practice. The injuries and soreness I was experiencing had nothing to do with how in shape I was; it was all due to competing at an elite level that my body just wasn't used to yet.

Chapter 81

I hobbled back down to breakfast the next morning. After a light breakfast, I was ready for our full-contact practice. I wasn't as sore as I was the night before, but I was still plenty sore. I made sure that my aches didn't impact my playing performance, though. As the day went on, I was eventually able to block a defender once or twice. Other linemen during practice were able to block the defender nearly every time, but I wasn't worried about what they could do; I was only worried about my personal progression.

As the week went on, I was getting more comfortable with practicing at this new level. My ability to block defenders continued to improve and I was able to stop the defenders on a more regular basis. Although I still wasn't quite at the backup level, I certainly had backup potential. Rather than being concerned with the nearly 40 players who were going to be cut at the end of the pre-season, I chose to focus on the five offensive linemen that would be sent home; that would decrease my competition by nearly 90%. I didn't get much time to play during our practices, but I felt that I was at least able to show how quickly I could progress in the short amount of time given.

By the second week of training camp, only five players had left the team voluntarily; all during the first day. Of those five, none of them came from the offensive line. I still had another week to be in the top half of the 10 of us eyeing a backup role on the offensive line. Not only was I improving in practice, but my ability to heal was improving as well. I was no longer going to bed in pain, my bruises healed, and my wounds closed faster. After a sore first week, I was able to practice the entire second week without any lingering injuries. My improved recovery time allowed me to practice at my full potential.

Finally, training camp was over. The veterans were happy because they were ready to start the season and felt training camp was a waste of their time. The younger guys were glad it was over because they were tired of being flopped around like rag dolls. I, personally, was a little disappointed it was over. I only had two weeks to show my talent, and I wanted more opportunity. But training camp would only be the beginning of a long summer.

Chapter 82

Our pre-season was only one third of the way complete at the end of camp. We still had four more weeks to display our talents before the coaches made their final cuts. We worked in our small groups during the first two days of practice, and in our large group during the second two. We would use Thursday as a full team scrimmage, and as a way for the coaches to set their depth chart. After two days off, we would be able to play in a full game. The practice schedule was nothing new to me, but the game at the end of the week would be a new experience.

Going into my first exhibition game, I was slated as the third-string center. At the college level, I wouldn't have seen any time as a third-stringer. During the exhibition games, however, I would be able to see more playing time. The exhibition games were similar to non-conference games. They were used as tune-up games to see which plays were successful, and what players would contribute the most. The exhibition games didn't count towards the season records, so coaches rarely played their starters once they determined who their starters would be.

Getting to the game was an experience of its own. The team actually flew us to those games, where we had a flock of supporters waiting for us at the airport. Before the season had even started, we were treated like celebrities by loyal fans. From the airport, we were shuttled to the hotel where the entire team was housed. The next morning, we were shuttled to the game on luxury busses and escorted into the locker room. The only time I had ever been treated like that was during the Major College Football Championship Game. The exhibition games were not championship games, though. They were simply scrimmages against another teams.

In the locker room, I expected the usual pre-game speech. Before that game, however, there was no speech. Apparently at the professional level, coaches never gave speeches because players were expected to be fired up on their own. Instead, Mike and I talked about our high school goal of playing professional football together. We had decided that even though we were technically playing in a professional exhibition game together, the game was merely a scrimmage and we still hadn't really achieved our goal yet of playing together in a pro game. We walked onto the field with the team. The field reminded me of the national championship game, except the arena wasn't nearly as full.

During the first half, I finally got called in to play in my first professional game. The play was simple, so I only had to worry about the defender across from me. Thanks in large part to the defender in practice, I was prepared for the guy who towered over me. As I snapped the ball, I stood up without fear and braced myself for a hard hit. That hit, however, never came from him; it came from me. The team we were playing against also had their third-stringers in, so the guy I was playing against was closer to my experience level. I was able to own him for the entire second half.

Chapter 83

I went into the next practice with more confidence after having played in my first professional football game. The offensive line coach still had me as a third-stringer, but treated all of us as if we were starters. He made it clear that even though his starters had been set, the rest of us would have to play at the same level of intensity as the other five positions were still open. That meant that I would have to play in the rest of the exhibition games as hard as I played in the first game. I would also have to use the following three weeks in practice to continue my progression as an elite player.

The second exhibition game was a home game. For that game, we were allowed to enjoy the previous night to ourselves, and only had to meet up with the team on game day. As we walked out of our home locker room on game day, I was hit with a mix of emotions. I was back on the same field where we had won a state championship for East Whitaker four years ago. It was exciting to be back, but this time, I was wearing the silver and gold of the Michigan Knights. The stadium wasn't as full, and the atmosphere wasn't as charged as our championship game, but I was still fired up because I would be playing on the field that I wanted to make my home for the next several years.

During that game, I received even less playing time than I had the week before because the starters were given even more time to play. The coaches wanted to make sure they had the right athletes as starters, and wanted to see their progress from the previous game. That gave the backups only two quarters to play. With the shorter time, I was only called in for the 4th quarter. For the second game in a row, I was able to successfully protect my quarterback.

After being impressed with my play in the first two games, the offensive line coach wanted to see how I did playing against defensive starters during the third game. He watched as I held up the defender every time in our previous exhibition games, but wanted to see if that was due to my personal strength, or just the weakness of my opponents. After a few plays, he realized that it was a mixture of both. I was able to stop the starting defender a few times, but not nearly as much as I was able to stop the third-stringers. The starter was a lot stronger than the third-stringers I was used to playing against during the previous games, but no stronger than my opponent in practice. Even in practice, though, I still wasn't at the point where I was stopping him every time.

The fourth game was much like the first two. I was able to stop the defender every time after being placed back onto the third-string team and was again able to play an entire half. Finally, after four weeks of practices, games, and celebrity status, it was time to see if I made the cut. Once again, I wasn't worried about the others getting cut on the team; only the ones in our offensive line group. Since the team would only need to cut 15 total players in the first round, our offensive line coach only had to cut one of us. It was obvious who his choice would be; he was the only one who couldn't adjust to the life of a professional football player.

We were presented with our second round of cuts a few days later. Because they were cutting another 22 players, our offensive line coach had to cut four more of us. That time, I didn't survive the cut. I was disappointed, but I had also expected the news. Anyway, my goal wasn't to make it to the regular team; my goal was to make it to the practice squad. After getting cut, I joined the 21 other players who got cut that day in a separate conference room. None of us knew who would be getting a second chance to make the team, or whose dreams would soon be crushed. After a few minutes of waiting patiently in a room full of upset, anxious, scared, and nervous football players, the head coach walked into the room. He explained that only eight of us would be allowed to come back the next day, while everyone else would have to wait another year to try again. As hoped for, I made it to the practice squad.

Chapter 84

Practices during the regular season were no longer held at the local college. Instead, they were located at the Knights' official training facility. The facility provided everything needed to run practices. There were numerous small meeting rooms for positional groups, two large meeting rooms for the entire team, a cafeteria just for the players and staff, a state-of-the-art weight lifting room, a separate room with cardio machines surrounded by an indoor track, and an indoor playing field so practices could be held no matter what the weather was. The practice days were shorter than the days at training camp, but more intense. Right at the beginning, the 8 of us on the practice squad were pulled together and briefed on our new roles.

We would be an important part of the team, without actually being on the team. Just like in college, we weren't allowed to attend any games with the team, and were used to help improve the regular team. However, there were numerous differences compared to college football. We would be working out every day with the regular roster players. We would be part of the same workouts that they were a part of. During practices, we would be used in various ways and we wouldn't have set positions. The practice squad wasn't just used to help the regular roster guys; it was also a way to develop younger players while stashing away guys to be used later in the season. Unfortunately, we would only be able to play on the practice squad for two years. And sadly, in those two years, we could be released at any point. The good news was that we would be making more than $6,000 a week. Although it seemed like a lot of money, we would only be paid during the season.

The coach then gave us more definitive roles. Four of us would be linemen. We would either be used as defenders to help with the offensive line, or as offenders to help with the defensive line. Two guys in the group were used as both running backs and middle linebackers. The last two guys would be used as wide receivers and defensive backs.

After that quick meeting, we joined the rest of the team on the indoor practice field. My group of linemen were asked to help out the defensive line. Just like in previous practices, we stood on the line of scrimmage and blocked the defenders from getting by us. It was fun because we were able to hit other people, while staying in our small groups. In college, we had only been allowed to go full-contact when working as a full team. After an hour of working with the defenders, we were sent to join the offensive line. It was now our goal to get past the offensive line at any cost. For me, it would be the first time playing as a defender in four years.

It wasn`t quite like riding a bike, but it didn't take long for me to feel comfortable at the defensive end spot. I knew where to stand, and I knew how to attack once the ball was snapped; what I forgot about was how to successfully get past the guy on the other side. Once I stood up, I got knocked back down. That fall brought a couple of thoughts to my mind, as I lied there peacefully. First, the last time I went against an offensive lineman was in high school. Although it was in the state championship game, it was nowhere near the elite level I was currently at. Second, I would have to remember to put my hands out and expect the lineman to be there, otherwise he would continue to dominate me. I would have to prepare for him and make a plan to get around him, just like I did as a

Hornet. My strength would have to be my biggest weapon once again. Finally, I would have to get back up. Just like in training camp, I would have to get up no matter how many times I fell down. I didn't expect myself to get past the guy much, but I did expect myself to get back up every time. And with that, I was ready for the next hit.

The rest of the practice was a struggle, but I didn't let it bother me. I knew I could get kicked off the practice squad at any time, but I also knew that the practice squad was used to develop new talent and the coaches were more interested in personal growth than failure. I would have to use the squad as an opportunity to get back into my defensive shape. I knew I wouldn't make the roster right away, but I also knew I only had two years to get there. After practice, we spent an hour in the weight room.

Chapter 85

  With the first day of regular-season practice out of the way, we had three more practice days left until the first game of the season. The second day was spent in our linemen group. Again, the offense worked separate from the defense, but we were able to work with both groups. I was more than comfortable as a center, and I was starting to get more comfortable as a defensive end. Even though I didn't get past the offensive tackle very often, I reminded myself that I was no longer on the college scout team.

  When I was on the scout team, it was our job to make our starters better football players. We would have to be perfect for them to get better at their position. If we did well, they did well. If we did poorly, we were off the team. As a practice squad member, however, there was less pressure. The guys on the regular roster would use other guys from the regular roster to practice on. We were more or less tackling dummies for the rest of the team. So even though I wasn't quite at my full potential as a defensive end, I didn't have to worry about my spot on the team because the offensive tackle would still be able to improve later in the week against the starting defensive end. I just had to make sure that I was constantly improving.

  By the third day of that week, we had a different assignment. While the team was working in a big group, the 8 of us blocked against each other on the line of scrimmage so that the kickers and punters could practice kicking during real-game situations. The task was easy because we didn't hit hard. The special teams coach simply wanted the kickers to work on kicking while feeling the pressure of the defenders coming at them. It got monotonous after two hours, but it gave us something different to do as members of the Michigan Knights.

At the end of the week, the team ran a scrimmage. There was a scorekeeper controlling the scoreboard, as well as the game clock. It was just like our spring game at USM, as players were hitting each other as hard as they could. Even the quarterback was getting hit during the scrimmage. The coaches allowed him to get hit because they would rather have him get hit during practice and learn, than to get hit during a game and lose. With the scrimmage going on, the 8 of us were left to be spectators.

After two days off, it was game day again. Unlike our pre-season games, we had to watch the game from home. With the extra day off, I was able to utilize our home gym. While working out, I was able to watch my new team play. It was cool seeing all of the familiar faces. When the game was over, the Knights had triumphed. It was the first time in five years that they were able to win their first game of the season. The victory could've been due to Mike's 2 touchdowns and 200 yards of rushing, but I gave all of the credit to the linemen; somebody had to.

Chapter 86

After the first game of the season, the practice schedule changed a bit. Because the game was on Sunday, we were given Monday off, allowing the team some time to recover. The first two days of practice that week would be spent reviewing game film in small groups, then working on correcting errors committed during the game. The third day was a walk-through day with the first half being spent in small groups, while the second half was a full team session. On Friday, the team ran through another exhibition-type scrimmage. The team would have only one more day off before game day. If the game was an away game, the day before and the day after the game were used as travel days.

As members of the practice squad, we were allowed to watch game film in any group of our choosing. It allowed us to better ourselves on the practice squad while progressing as players trying to make the regular team. I chose to watch film with the defensive line because, not only did I need to spend most of my time working on defense, but I had also re-kindled my passion for the position.

In our Tuesday and Wednesday practice sessions, our group continued to help the offensive and defensive lines. We conducted the same drills as usual, but ran them more effectively as we were becoming stronger players. On Thursday, we assisted with the walk-throughs in both the big and small groups. But on Friday, we again watched from the sidelines. The schedule remained constant for the rest of the season, while our group of 8 remained intact. None of us were kicked off the team during the season, but none of us were called up either. As players got injured, they were replaced by one of us during practices. By Sunday, however, our team had usually traded players with other teams to replace the injured player.

When I wasn't practicing, I was at home. I spent the time either working out, or working with Christine on the plans for the wedding. She loved her job as a teacher, and was making good money at it. She had nights and weekends off, which allowed us to spend more time together. We especially loved our Sundays because, after a nice breakfast prepared by his personal chef, we would watch Mike play.

Not all of Mike's games were like his first, but he did manage to rush for over 1,000 yards that season. He also averaged almost one touchdown per game. His averages didn't quite give him all-star status, but they certainly justified his starting role. He was, however, disappointed in his performance during the season and felt responsible for the Knights not making it to the playoffs.

Even though the Knights missed the playoffs by only 2 games that season, they still had a better record than the previous year. After a long season of 16 regular season games, I would call it a successful season overall. I became even more comfortable at defense and wanted to play the following season more than ever.

Chapter 87

While I was earning it, $6,000 a week seemed like a lot of money. Once the season was over, though, I had no income. Fortunately, we were living with Mike at no cost. Unfortunately, we had a wedding, a honeymoon, and a future home of our own to pay for. I saved my money as I earned it on the team, but it wasn't enough to cover everything. We decided that with the money Christine was bringing in, I would only have to work a short-term job to make up for our additional income needs.

I had a degree in business, but didn't worry about using it right away as I only needed a temporary job until the season started back up. At the suggestion of many of the guys on the team, I decided to apply for a job as a security guard. During my interview, the employer was excited about my size, and knew it would be an asset. He wasn't too happy that I would be leaving at the end of June, but understood when I told him why. The job wasn't a glory job, but it paid enough during those six months to supplement our income. I especially made my co-workers happy, who were able to brag that they were making $10 an hour alongside a real Michigan Knight.

Mike, however, used the off-season to recover. He had many friends from the team to hang out with, but never had any serious girlfriends. He told us that he didn't want to get into a big relationship because most girls seemed to only be attracted his money. He did, however, offer to give us some of his money to help with our plans, but we told him sharing his house with us had been more than enough.

Finally, on May 18th, our wedding day came. With Mike at my side, and Christine's sister at hers, we were officially married. After a wonderful ceremony, we had a fun reception, celebrating with our family and close friends. I wanted to invite the whole team, but I knew I couldn't afford the food bill. At the end of a long party, we jumped into the car and were off on our honeymoon.

My boss was kind enough to give me a week off from work. We decided to make the most of that time and took a long road trip. With money tight, we couldn't afford a fancy trip, so we were happy just to spend the time together in the car on a 2-day trip to the Atlantic Ocean. Seeing the ocean was amazing. As we stared into the large body of water, we realized just how small we were compared to the rest of the world. A month later, I finished my career as a security guard. At the end of June, I turned in my badge and turned up the intensity; it was time to get back to work.

Chapter 88

Training camp was much easier the second time around. Not only was I prepared for those two weeks, but I was also in better shape. The two weeks seemed to fly by as I already knew what to expect, and the pressure of making the team wasn't as intense as it had been the previous season. I knew that all I had to do was keep up with the rest of the guys and let my play during the exhibition games determine my status on the team. Just like with the previous season, I used the two hours of hitting after lunch as my opportunity to show off my experience as an offensive lineman.

In those practices after lunch, I was having a lot more success against the guys on the team. I could feel myself getting stronger, and I was no longer intimidated by my competition. I continued to stick with the offensive line because I was still more comfortable as a center than I was as a defensive end. I made it clear just how comfortable I was, too. During training camp, I gave the defender a good fight every time the ball was snapped.

Although my performance on the offensive line was improving, I still didn't get off the third-string team. I had a year of experience under my belt, and got stronger, but my practice opponents had also gotten stronger and gained more experience as well. To make matters worse, the team picked more offensive linemen during the Selection Showcase during the off-season, which gave me even more competition.

During the four exhibition games, I fought even harder than I did in practice. As a third-stringer, I was allowed to play as much as I had the previous season. Again, I was playing against other third-stringers, so my level of success seemed phenomenal. After those four exhibition games were over, we were called in for our group meeting to discuss the cuts.

While waiting for the results to come in, I briefly reflected on my progress during the pre-season. I was defiantly getting stronger and felt more comfortable playing at the professional level. I went through all of the exhibition games without letting the defender beat me on the line, but I didn't get very many matches against the defense. I did have a year of experience, however, I spent that previous season on the practice squad and didn't get the experience of playing against real opponents during real games. After reflecting, I came to the conclusion that I would no doubt end up spending another season on the practice squad.

My thoughts were quickly interrupted by the offensive line coach. As predicted, I made the cut of 75. At that cut, the line coach got rid of two linemen. A few days later, the offensive line coach only needed to get rid of three players. For a second straight year, I didn't make the 53 man roster. As I left the room with the other cut players, the line coach pulled me to the side and told me that I would have a better season the upcoming year. That comment made me curious, as I couldn't figure how another year on the practice squad could get better. It would be a few months before I got my answer.

Chapter 89

That year, the team did a complete turn-around from the previous season. The year before, the team was only two wins away from making it to the playoffs. This year, the team only had two wins going into the last game of the regular season. The coaches never told us why we were doing so poorly, but the media certainly had their opinions. In the evenings, I would read the newspaper in an effort to understand what was happening to our team.

The sports reporters believed that we were so dedicated to the run that we forgot to work on our other weapons (like defense). Mike got the ball a lot, but he was the only one getting the ball, according to the newspaper. It made it really easy for the teams playing us because all they had to do was put a little more attention on him, and less attention on the rest of our offensive. Unfortunately, no matter how much he scored, with a bad defense, the other teams had no problems scoring more. Finally, after much speculation in the papers, the coaches spoke out about the team's hardships.

After 14 regular season games, the head coach brought us together for a team meeting. He finally admitted that the papers were right in calling our defense horrible and the reason for us not winning games. Even though there were only two games left in the season, the coach was going to make a drastic change right away. He then introduced us to the new defensive coach. The new coach announced that he would spend the week observing our defense and attempt to create a better attack plan for us. The next week, we would put that plan into action and use it during the last game of the season. Before we left the room, he made it clear that none of our defenders were safe.

A week later, our new defensive coach followed through with his plan. In the beginning of the season, teams were able to trade their players for players from other teams. Unfortunately, that process was only available during the first half of the season, so teams were unable to trade during the second half. Instead, the new defensive coach simply exchanged players on the defense with players from the practice squad. Not everyone from our squad got the promotion, so I knew my hard work on the team was finally paying off when I got called up to the regular roster team.

The coach wanted me as a defensive lineman. He was impressed with how well I had progressed during practices, and how well I was able to keep up with the starters on the team. He didn't want me as a starter, though, because the starting defensive linemen were going to stay where they were. Instead, he wanted me as a backup because the backup defensive end was about to find his way off the team. I spent the rest of the week practicing with the real team. Thanks to my time working with this defensive line, I was already familiar with the plays and the players, and I already had experience in working against the starting offensive linemen. The practices that week simply gave me extended time on the field to get used to working *with* the roster team, instead of working *against* them.

Chapter 90

After watching 31 games from home, I was finally able to watch a Michigan Knights' regular season game from the sideline. The game was a home game, so I was used to the atmosphere of our home stadium. It was even less intimidating than the exhibition games I was used to because the stands were even less full during that game. I guess fans had stopped showing up when their team had won only two games. With plenty of room in the stadium, I had no problem getting tickets for my wife and parents.

As a backup lineman in college, I was used to watching the game from the sideline because backups weren't used very often. At the professional level, however, backup players were used all the time on defense. In the pros, coaches wanted the linemen to play as hard as they could for every play, but knew that would cause exhaustion. To alleviate the tiredness, defensive players were allowed to rest for a few plays, so that they could come back into the game fresh. As a spectator at home, I knew that backups were used often, but I was still surprised when the defensive coach called me in.

We were playing against the Florida Pythons in the last game of the season. They already had a spot in the playoffs, so they were benching their star players. Even though I would be trying to take down a second-string running back and quarterback, I would still have to get through their first-string offensive line because they didn't get the game off. Out of the huddle, I stood in my new defensive end position. Once the ball was snapped, I was ready for the offensive tackle coming at me. Thanks to two years of hard work in practice against our starting offensive tackles, I was ready for him. There was a little struggle, but

I got by him. Once I did, I found the running back and took him down. After that play, the defender I relieved was ready to come back in. On my way back to the sidelines, the new coach came over to me and shook my hand. He knew how hard I had been working at practice and was excited to see that his new attack plan was really working.

As the game went on, our defense was able to keep the Pythons from scoring, and I was able to take down the running back two more times. Towards the end of the game, as our defense was getting ready for yet another drive, I got called back in. The time was running down, so we knew they would be trying hard to score as quickly as possible. Because they didn't have much time, we were expecting their quarterback to throw the ball as far as he could down the field. That meant the quarterback would be the only one behind the offensive line, as he would send everyone else out to catch the ball. As defensive linemen, our only objective for that play was to tackle the quarterback as hard and as fast as we could.

There were five offensive linemen blocking our four defensive linemen, yet somehow three of us were able to break through the line. With three big guys coming at him, the quarterback panicked. He was already facing my direction, so I was able to lock eyes with him as I came at him. With the quarterback locked on me, he had no idea that there was another defender coming from behind him. The quarterback knew he couldn't afford to get sacked, so as he was being thrown down to the ground, he quickly got rid of the ball. Unfortunately for him, he threw the ball too late and it didn't quite make it past my outstretched hands. Instinct took over as I grabbed the ball out of the air and ran the other direction for a touchdown.

It was only our third win of the season, but the team was still excited. After 15 games, our team finally had a solid defense again. Our head coach did the right thing by getting a new defensive coach during the season, and the new coach did the right thing by trusting in me. After two hours of celebrating with our families and teammates outside of the stadium, Mike, Christine and I went home to celebrate on our own. That day, I played my first game as a Michigan Knight, and scored my first touchdown as a professional football player. Even though it was one of the greatest days of my playing career, Christine had news that made that day 10 times better. Nine months later, our family would be growing by one.

Chapter 91

Once the season was over, I went right back to my temporary job as a security guard. I knew it would be my last year on the force because, after training camp, I would either be on the regular roster, or start looking for a real job. Christine and I also started looking for a house of our own. Even though Mike's house was big enough for all of us, we wanted to raise a child in our own home. After a few months of looking, we finally found a modest house within our price range. The house was a few miles away from Mike's, so we would still be able to spend plenty of time with him.

With the team's horrible season, Mike worked out harder than usual during the off-season. We both wanted to contribute to the team, but we had different ideas of how to do so. He made it his goal to rush for over 1,500 yards, while carrying the team back into playoff contention. My goal was to make a considerable impression during training camp and try to make it on the regular roster because I would not be eligible to play on the practice squad for a third year. I knew the new defensive coach had been impressed by my performance the previous season, but I also knew that he was planning on continuing to make bigger changes to the team.

The team never communicated to its players what changes they made during the off-season, so it was up to us to find out on our own. Just like I did during the previous season, I got most of my information from the newspaper. Apparently, as soon as the season was over, the team got rid of more than half of their starting defensive players. Most of those guys were traded to other teams for picks in the Selection Showcase.

During Selection Showcase Week, teams were given one pick per round, for a total of seven picks. Teams were allowed, however, to use any of their picks to barter with other teams. Teams would generally trade their picks for one or more players from another team. The traded player's value usually correlated with which round the pick came from. So if a team was willing to trade a high-caliber athlete, they would expect to receive a pick from the first round in return. If, however, the player wasn't as talented, they would expect to receive a pick from the sixth or seventh round. After trading some of their players to other teams, the Knights were able to score additional picks in the first, third, and fourth round of Selection Showcase.

In addition to those multiple picks, the Knights also earned the first pick due to their poor record. With their second overall pick, the team chose a very talented wide receiver. They then used the rest of their picks to build up their defense. By the end of the selection process, most of the players who had been cut by the team at the end of the season had been replaced by younger players who had the potential to develop into high-caliber athletes.

After Selection Showcase Week, the Knights continued to trade more of their players to other teams. They traded some of their high-priced athletes for multiple athletes from other teams. For the price of one defender, the Knights were able to receive two or three affordable defenders who hadn't quite developed yet, but still had potential for growth. So when it was all said and done, the Knights had gotten rid of most of their veterans for a bunch of young defenders who would be competing with me for a spot on the regular roster.

Chapter 92

Going into training camp my third year, I was left with one final chance to make the team. My only chance of making the roster team would be to have the best training camp of my life. My advantage was my experience with the team; my touchdown during the previous season didn't hurt. My disadvantage was the many new faces on the team, and the experiences they had playing for other teams.

After our first big team meeting, we met in our positional groups. That year, rather than working out with the offense, I worked with the defense. The group wasn't any different than the offensive line group, but the numbers were a little different. During the regular season, the team would have eight defensive linemen on the roster. In the room that day were 14 players fighting it out to make the team. That meant six players would have to be cut at the end of summer. When I was in the offensive line group, the coach had already made up his mind for starters, so there were less of us fighting for fewer backup spots. With the new defensive coach and his new action plan, though, nobody was guaranteed a starting spot so all 14 of us were fighting for a starting role.

During the full-contact practice, I was able to use my strength and speed against the new guys on the team. I felt confident as I was able to keep up with all of them. Because there were very few veterans in our group, our whole group worked to their full potential for the entire two weeks. Most of us received at least one injury, but we all bounced back and survived the full-contact practices. By the end of the training camp, all 14 of us were still on the team, and still itching for a position.

We waited anxiously as the defensive line coach announced who would be starting during our first exhibition game. Everybody had the same chance of playing, so nobody was sure of their place on the team. We were waiting like lottery ticket holders waiting for their numbers to be drawn, as the coach began his announcements. After the first, second, and third-string players had been announced, there were only two of us left; a player from last years practice squad and me.

After the first exhibition game, the new defensive line coach decided to switch up our lines again. The coach put me on the second-string with three other players from last season's team. The mix-up confused all of us as we couldn't understand what happened in the first game to create such drastic changes. The coach explained to us that he had only four games to figure out who his starting defensive line was going to be. Since nobody was guaranteed a spot, everybody would have to rotate through the lines so that we would all have a fair opportunity to audition.

By the end of the four games, I was able to play in each group. After not playing at all during the first game, I was able to record 3 tackles in the second game while on the third-string. As a second-stringer, I added another 2 tackles. When I finally got my chance to start in the 4th game, I had an outstanding 4 tackles; 1 of those being a sack. I don't know if it was the excitement of finally being a starter, or if my hard work was paying off, but that last game as a starter was my best game ever. After four exhibition games, I even had the most tackles among defensive linemen.

Chapter 93

My time on the practice squad, as well as my time in the weight room, allowed me to get back into my comfort zone with defense. During the exhibition games, I felt like I was back in high school again and was riding a huge wave of momentum. I knew I would be able to get impressive numbers once I got my comfort level back up. If it weren't for the new defensive coach, though, I wouldn't have had a shot at playing as much as I did during exhibition games. Even though I was looking good out there, however, I was still competing against guys who had always looked good on the field, and had been playing defense a lot longer than I had. Needless to say, I knew my rejuvenation on defense would be enough to make the first cut, but I wasn't as sure about the second.

Days later, I experienced something new. My name was announced as a regular roster player. Finally! I didn't have to awkwardly leave the room as a cut player. The defensive line coach had been very impressed with my performance during the exhibition games, and was excited about my constant progress. He said I wasn't quite ready to be a starter, but I definitely had the potential to start the following season as long as I kept improving. The other three backup players were new to the team. As it turned out, the defensive coach wanted all of his young players to start as backups, and slowly work their way into starting roles as they became more comfortable playing at the professional level.

As a backup in the pros, I knew my life was going to change. First of all, I would be able to reap the benefits of being on the roster team. I would be able to watch the games from the sideline and travel with the team, my name would be in the program sold to fans at games, and my family would receive free tickets to all of our home games. Also, I would be receiving a significant pay increase. My $6,000 a week would turn into a $500,000 for one season. I've never had that kind of money in my life, let alone in one year. Finally, Mike and I were one week away from achieving our high school goal; after seven years, we would finally be playing together in the pros.

In the first week of regular-season practice, our head coach spent a lot of time walking us through plays. The team wanted to use that season as a rebuilding year, so the coach didn't mind spending extra time at practice helping out the young talent. He was more concerned about the long-term value of the team, and less concerned about the current season. I loved it because we were able to use the time in practice as more of a learning process. I was already used to the team's plays, but I wasn't used to being in them. Walking through the plays allowed me to get used to my role as a defensive end without worrying about someone trying to hit me. I knew if I appreciated it, the rest of the young guys did too. Even the veterans were treated like they were new to the team. They didn't mind because, over the course of many years, they too were tired of getting beaten up.

Our last day of practice was by no means a walk-through, though. The head coach retained the tradition of using the last day of the week as a scrimmage day. We were all expected to hit as hard as we could, while flawlessly executing our new plays at full-speed. It took a while, but eventually we were all running at full speed, hitting at full strength, and executing the plays without error. Finally, after a long summer, and a long week of walk-throughs during practice, we were starting to look like a solid team.

Chapter 94

I felt my heart race as Mike and I walked onto that field together. We had finally accomplished a dream that took so long to achieve. It wasn't long before I had my first opportunity to play during the first game of the season. The defensive coach, as part of his new plan, wanted his backups to play as often as possible. He wanted to keep his starters fresh, while allowing the backups to get plenty of exposure to real games. Because of this, I was able to play nearly half of the game and was responsible for 4 of our defensive tackles. The rest of the defenders also had great numbers but, unfortunately, it wasn't enough to stop our opponent from scoring more than us.

Mike also had a great game. For him to achieve his goal of rushing for over 1,500 yards, he had to average just under 100 yards per game. He came close to that number, but their defense was too much for him. The wide receiver we picked up in the Selection Showcase was a young player, so he was still adjusting to the professional level. He caught a few catches, but not enough for the other team to divide their coverage between the receiver and the running back. Even though it wasn't Mike's best game as a running back, it was still a game that we would never forget; our first professional football game playing together.

The following two games were even more successful for us. I totaled 6 tackles in those games, while Mike averaged 100 yards and 2 touchdowns. The receiver was starting to get better, so the defenders had to protect both him and Mike at the same time. Additionally, our defense was getting better, and we even managed to win one of those two games.

On September 21st, our little baby boy, Alan, was born. I've had many proud moments as a player, but that was my proudest moment ever as a father. There were so many people in the hospital room visiting him that the hospital wanted to start selling tickets to get in. Sadly, the next day, I had to board the team plane for our next game. I hated to leave because I wanted to spend the rest of my life holding that child and his mother, but there I was; away from them after Alan's first day of life. I was so focused on life at home that my life on the field began to suffer. The offensive tackle held me up so much at the beginning of the game that I eventually had to sit the bench for the rest of the game.

Losing that game gave our team had a record of 2-2. The coaches liked our progress on defense, however, and even felt that we were progressing faster than expected. The defensive coach felt his players were adapting well to the changes and wouldn't need to be replaced during the game as often. With the horrible timing of my poorly played game, I was no longer seen as a starting contender, and any chance I had at starting was gone. I would still be able to play as a backup, but I would spend most of the game watching from the sidelines. My performance during that game may have been the reason why I wasn't promoted, but being there for my son's birth was worth giving up some playing time.

I continued to watch the game from the sidelines and eventually my playing time gradually increased. I made the most of small amount of playing time I got and was able to record the 3rd most tackles on the defensive line. Meanwhile, Mike was just over 100 yards shy of achieving his 1,500 yard goal, going into the last game of the season. That game would end up making an impact on both of our careers.

Chapter 95

We had a mediocre year, so we clearly weren't the best team in our division. However, with an impressive win streak in the middle of the season, accompanied by some timely loses by other teams in our conference, we were playing for one of the two wild-card spots in the post-season playoffs. All we had to do was win our last game. Our team had a lot on the line.

Going into halftime, the game was tied. Mike had rushed for only 53 yards and had yet to cross the goal line. Surprisingly enough, it was our defense that kept us in the game, as both teams only had one touchdown each. After a long season of ironing out wrinkles, our defense was finally solid enough to compete against any team in the league. As long as we could continue to hold those guys for one more half, all we needed was one more score to go to the playoffs.

In the 4th quarter, we got the score we were looking for. The score came from Mike's 80-yard touchdown scamper, putting him well over 1,500 yards. All we had to do now was keep them from scoring to win the game. With our much-improved defense, we knew it was a task we could easily handle. The defensive coach went back to his plan of keeping the defensive line fresh, so he continued to rotate us through on a more regular basis. With less than a minute to play, it was my turn.

The other team was 60 yards away from tying up the game. When their quarterback called for the ball, we saw the center snap it, but we never saw the quarterback move. As I was trying to get past the offensive line, I saw the football lying at my feet. I was no longer worried about getting past the offensive line; my instinct kicked in and I jumped on the ball. As soon as I landed on it, I had an entire field of football players on me. As more opponents jumped on, I could feel my arms getting pinched by other players. I felt their punches to my kidneys. They were trying to inflict so much pain on me that I would focus more on self-preservation and less on the ball. What they didn't know was I had been through enough pain during my career that I wasn't going to let a pinched arm or a body punch get in the way of keeping that ball safe. With the ball back in our possession, we were able to run the clock down to finish the game. And suddenly, our rebuilding year turned into a playoff run.

Chapter 96

Being 1 of 12 teams in the playoffs was an honor; being 1 of 53 players to play for our team was a dream come true. I retained my role as a backup defensive end, and was able to contribute 2 tackles in the game. Mike continued to run the ball well, and scored 2 touchdowns. Unfortunately, those 2 touchdowns weren't enough as we lost to the team that would go on to win the championship game. Even though we lost the game, it was still one of my favorite games and I enjoyed every part of it.

During the off-season, I was able to spend plenty of time with my family. With the money I earned as a professional football player, I no longer needed a second job during the off-season. I was able to play the game I loved so much, and was paid more money than I knew what to do with. I was too busy during the season to spend any of it, so after paying off our house, we put the rest of the money away for our future. We had decided early that we weren't going to blow it all, because we didn't know if there would be more money coming the next year. Christine enjoyed her teaching job and still continued to work for the love of the job, while I spent my down time keeping in shape.

A week into the off-season, I heard some news that would no doubt impact my playing status on the team. Right after the season was over, two of our defensive ends decided to retire. They were getting older and weren't enjoying the game as much as they used to. They had both planned on leaving a season earlier, but after only winning three games that season, they decided to stay another year; not wanting to go out as losers. With those two players leaving, there would now be two openings on the starting defensive line.

Months later, as I watched the Selection Showcase Week on television, I wanted to see how the Knights were going to fill the void left by those two defensive linemen. During the 1st round, we picked up a center. In the 2nd and 3rd rounds, we picked up two wide receivers, and in the 4th round, a kicker. In the final three rounds, we continued to pick up more offensive players. At the conclusion of Selection Showcase Week, our team had not picked up any defensive replacements.

I continued to read the sports section daily to see if the Knights would trade some of their players for additional defensive ends. After a month, however, they weren't any trades. It didn't take a rocket scientist to do the math on this one. The Michigan Knights lost two starters on the defensive line. They had seven chances of picking up talented college athletes to fill the void, but went with offensive players instead. They then had two months to trade some of their players in the hopes of getting defensive linemen to take the starting role, but chose not to. As a result, I would be walking into training camp with the exact same group of defensive guys from the previous year. With no additional competition to worry about, and with two newly available spots on the defensive line, I would no longer be fighting to make the team; I would be fighting for a starting role.

Chapter 97

Training camp certainly had a different feel by my fourth year. I was really starting to feel like a veteran, even though it was just my second season off the practice squad. I was well aware of the camp schedule, and already knew what to expect. The meetings were more challenging for me since all of the plays presented were identical to the ones used the previous years, making it a struggle to stay awake. Again, I knew my primary objective would have to be using the two hours of hitting practice after lunch to prove my worth.

In those sessions, I knew I would have to be the best one on the field. I would have to use every minute I had to earn one of the starting spots. The defensive coach was left with a bunch of young guys who all spent a year developing into the athletes he wanted. That put us all pretty much on the same page, and with the same opportunity to become a star. Fortunately, I was used to playing against starting linemen, I had my plays memorized and I was in great shape. Unfortunately, so was everybody else.

In college, I was able to use my memorization skills as my biggest weapon to stand out from the guys who were stronger than me. During my first year on the practice squad, I was able to use my strength as my best weapon to get past the offensive tackle. With this group of guys who were as strong as me, as mean as me, and who knew the plays as well as I did, I didn't know what my secret weapon would be. Then, it dawned on me. In the pros, a defensive lineman wasn't judged by how well he knew the plays, or how strong he was; he was simply judged by how many tackles he contributed to the team. At the end of the previous season, I had the 3rd most tackles of any defensive lineman on the team. Additionally, I was smart enough to jump on the fumble that took us to the playoffs. I would have to ride that momentum and hope the coaches remembered my contributions to the previous season.

With my new thinking, I was able to worry less about my competitors, and focus more on my individual work. I began the camp in the best shape of my life, yet I continued to get stronger in those two weeks. During the hitting sessions, I barely struggled against the offensive tackle across from me, nor did I get winded during our speed and conditioning drills. I was having the best training camp of my life.

Mike, of course, had it a lot easier than I did. With his impressive run last season, he was guaranteed a spot on the team for the next five seasons. After his first season on the team, the general manager was so impressed with his running ability, that he guaranteed him a spot on the team for three seasons and would pay him a total of $12 million. At the conclusion of the previous season, his three years had expired so he was given a new contract which would keep him on the team for five years and paid him $5 million a season. Since the team was spending so much money on him, he knew he would start no matter how poorly he performed during camp.

Chapter 98

We never talked about how much money either one of us made; I just knew that he made a lot of money. But once I read about his new contract in the paper, it made sense why the starting players didn't play much during exhibition games. Simply put, teams didn't want to lose any money by injuring their star players during scrimmages. Once the teams knew who their starters would be, it was up to the backup players to play out the rest of the game. The concept made sense when I was making $6,000 a week and was playing nearly half of the exhibition games. It made less sense as I was standing on the sidelines with Mike for most of the exhibition season.

Our annual roster announcements were made a few days before the first exhibition game was set to kickoff. For the first game, I wasn't surprised to hear the defensive line coach call my name as a starter. I figured that the defensive coach was going to do what he did the previous year; give everybody a shot at starting. In my first game, I had a couple of good tackles before sitting out of the game for three quarters. Going into the second game, the defensive line coach declared me a starter for yet a second straight game. A few days later, he called me into his office to talk. He told me that he liked the way I had improved over the course of three seasons on the Michigan Knights. He had watched me come in as a center who barely made the practice squad, and turn into a defensive end who helped take us to the playoffs. Because of my work, determination, ability to progress, and commitment to the team, he wanted to give me a shot at starting during all of the exhibition games, with the reminder that it was mine to lose.

I loved being a starter at first. I was treated with respect on the team, and had more confidence than I had money. But as the exhibition games went on, I was beginning to feel disappointed. I loved the game of football, but I loved playing it even more. Unfortunately, I spent most of the exhibition games on the sidelines, where I had watched the games as a backup for half of my football life. I suddenly felt like I was being punished for being a starter. I wasn't making that much money on the team, so why couldn't I go out there and hit somebody?

By the third exhibition game, after hearing me complain for the last time, Mike told me to snap out of it. He reminded me that the defensive line coach had told me this was mine to lose. If I survived the exhibition games and continued to play the only way I knew how, I would have a career as a starter on my favorite professional football team. With less time on the playing field, I had less of an opportunity to screw up. All of the sudden, I loved the sidelines.

At the conclusion of the exhibition games, I racked up 10 tackles in the short amount of playing time. It was no surprise that I made it to the 53 man roster. What did surprise me was my meeting with the general manager. I didn't know what to expect as I walked into the boss's office for the first time. In high school, a meeting with the principal was never good. I had only met the general manager once, so I knew the meeting was either really good, or really bad. As I sat down, he got right into it. He told me he had good news and better news. The good news was, as a starter, he wanted to raise my pay to $1 million for the upcoming season. The better news was, if I had a successful season, they would give me a big contract that would guarantee me a place on the team for a few more seasons, while making a lot more money, and even a bonus just for signing the contract.

Chapter 99

I went on a spending spree the next day. I flew my parents, Christine's parents, and even Mike's parents in to Lansing so that we could all celebrate together. I even invited the other three players that would be starting on the line with me. We had a lot to celebrate. First of all, Mike and I would both be making a lot of money. Second of all, we would both be starting on our favorite team. Third, and best of all, after seven long years, the two of us would not only be playing on the same team together; we would both be starting on a professional football team that had a good chance to win the playoffs.

All of our parents stayed in town to watch the Michigan Knight's home opener. It was a game that everybody was excited about. After declaring the previous season a "rebuilding season", we came back and made it to the playoffs. That season, we had a defense full of young players with very little experience, and an offense fueled by only one running back. This season, our defense had gained a year of experience after finally shaping in to a solid unit, while our offense gained an additional weapon. After a season of no expectations, who knew what we were capable of in a season with high expectations?

As we rushed onto the field in our silver and gold home uniforms, The "Kingdome" erupted. Prior to that season, our stadium was simply known as the place where the Michigan Knights played their home games, and was named after a company that paid a lot of money to sponsor us. But the general manager wanted to add hype to the already-hyped season. He talked the sponsor into naming the arena "THE KINGDOME... presented by 'Some Company That Paid a Lot of Money'. He then spent a lot of money on changing the interior so that it looked like we were battling our opponents in a jousting arena during the Renaissance Era. They even served turkey legs without silverware, just like they would at a Medieval Times restaurant.

With the team's high expectations, a solid defense, a heavily armored offense, and an arena disguised as an event known for its beheadings, the anticipation for kickoff was intense. Finally, as the ball was kicked into the end zone by our new kicker, numerous cameras flashed and we were ready to go to work. Since our opponent had the ball first, I would waste no time as a starter. The very first play of the season would end with a tackle behind the line of scrimmage, compliments of yours truly. After stopping the offense from gaining 10 yards, it was our turn with the ball. Once Mike broke free for a 75-yard dash, the game broke open. Granted, we were playing the worst team in the league, we were still more than happy to take the 28-point win.

As we ran off the field, we were overwhelmed by sports reporters. I was used to them on the field, I was used to them talking to Mike, but I was not used to them talking to me. They really had no idea who I was, or where I came from, but they were impressed with my 3 sacks and 7 tackles. I knew I wouldn't have that kind of game every time, but I was more than willing to soak in the 15 minutes of fame while it lasted. By the end of the day, they predicted I would break the record in tackles by defensive linemen, while Mike would break 2,000 yards. He was already 1,700 yards away from it.

Chapter 100

My 15 minutes of fame stretched into a week. After the game, I was surrounded by local media. By the end of the week, I was talking to national outlets. They were really interested in my earth-shattering game, but they were even more interested in the story of how Mike and I started as high school nobodies, and turned into gridiron heroes for the Michigan Knights. Some of the stations briefly mentioned us, while others had special segments dedicated to us. Even in practice, we had reporters waiting for us. I didn't let it interfere with my practices, though; if anything, I used the attention to enhance my practices. If they were only there for my high-caliber playing ability, I would have to maintain that ability in order to stay in the papers.

Practice was no different as a starter than it was as a backup. I was treated the same during practices, and had to run the same plays. I knew that in practice, everyone was expected to perform at starting-level performance, even those on the practice squad, so that any one player could be used during any play of any game. Although I was held to higher expectations as a starter, I had already kept myself to those higher expectations during the previous three seasons on the team.

We ran onto the field, ready for another home game after a hard week of practice. The atmosphere was even more electric. The team was led onto the field by two white horses ridden by two knights in silver armor. The game started just like the first one did; we kept the other team from scoring and countered with a score of our own. Even our new kicker was looking good after not missing a single point. Even though we won the game, our stats weren't quite what they were the previous game. Mike only came up with 100 yards, while I managed to tackle the ball carrier 4 times.

I anticipated another flock of sports reporters as we headed into the locker room after the game. However, the only cameras I saw were the ones surrounding our new kicker. After we changed into our street clothes, I was still expecting reporters to be waiting for us outside the locker room; once again, they were nowhere to be found. After going through most of the week without seeing the media, Mike finally explained why. When an athlete had an out-of-this-world game, the media was all over them; but when the athlete finally came back down to earth, the cameras were gone.

The media left us alone for most of the season, but caught right back up with us at our last game of the season. Going into that game, I had been averaging 4 tackles per game and was leading all defensive linemen in the league. Meanwhile, Mike was closing in on two major milestones. The first was touchdowns in a season; he only needed 2 more touchdowns to break the league record. The second milestone was yards. He was less than 60 yards away from being 1 of 5 players ever to rush for over 2,000 yards in a single season. We were nearly guaranteed success because we were playing the South Dakota Mountaineers, the team that we embarrassed in week one.

After the game, we were again surrounded by cameras and reporters. As predicted, Mike had broken the season record with 30 touchdowns, while entering the 2,000-yard club. Meanwhile, I recorded 5 tackles that game, which gave me the most tackles as a defensive lineman in the professional league. Oh, and by the way, we also helped our team win the division for the first time in nearly two decades.

Chapter 101

One benefit of having the second best record in our conference was that we were given the first week off, while the other four teams played the first round. Our team, and the team with the best record in the conference, would play the two winners from round one. If we won that game in round two, we moved on to play the remaining team in round three. A win there would put us in the Professional Football League's Showdown Game against the round three winner from the other conference in our league. So, not only did we get an extra week to prepare and heal, but we were also one round closer to being champions.

After their near-upset in round one, we were faced with the Florida Pythons in round two. I was very familiar with the Pythons, as they were the team that gave me my first professional football touchdown. I also remembered them as the team that had already been in the playoffs the previous season and were used to winning. We were riding the momentum of one of our best seasons, but they were riding the momentum of five consecutive successful seasons. None of that really mattered. All we had to do was beat them once to eliminate them from the playoffs.

We hit them hard with our running back, and followed that up with our wide receiver. They were able to counter with a wide receiver of their own, and a defense that couldn't be beat. At halftime, we heard something new. We were down by 10 points while in the locker room and were soon listening to a halftime pep-talk delivered by one of the players. It was the first time I had heard a locker room speech as a pro football player, but it was definitely needed. We were reminded of how far we had come and how quickly we had turned around. We should've been proud to be where we were at, but we should NOT be willing to simply accept the loss. He told us that we could, as a team, beat them and take this game. For the first time I could remember, Mike was able to inspire others by his words, not just by his running ability.

We needed that speech, but it didn't seem to make a difference; their lead only got bigger. However, like Mike said, we had the right to be proud just for making it to the second round of the playoffs. As the rounds went on, we watched the tournament from home. For the second season in a row, we lost to a team that ended up as the season champion. I guess there wasn't much shame in that. At least it gave us a new goal for the following year.

A few days before the Showdown Game, two major announcements were made. The first regarded the player of the year awards. Those awards were given to the best offensive player, the best defensive player, the best rookie, and the best overall player from that given season. With his phenomenal performance with the ball, Mike was given the Offensive Player of the Year and the League MVP award. With my incredible amount of tackles, I was given the Defensive Player of the Year Award. The second announcement was that we had both been selected as players on the Professional Football League's All-Star Game roster.

Chapter 102

I was married to the love of my life, who gave me my son, Alan. I was able to make a lot of money, while I played the sport I loved so much, with the friend I grew up with. I had the best season of my life, and was getting ready for the biggest contract of my life. And if that wasn't enough, we were getting ready to play on one of the biggest stages in professional football with some of the biggest names in the game. Mike and I were now considered all-stars.

Mike and I were both selected to play on the same team, marking our fourth different team together. A week after the Showdown Game, we were flown out to sunny California with our families to partake in the week-long festivities. We all flew to the Pacific Ocean in first class. When we landed, we were given a day to ourselves so that we could be tourists in the state. We ended the day on the beach watching the sunset. Even though Mike and I still had a lot of football life ahead of us, we took a second to reflect on the journey we had endured.

The next morning was the first day of practice for the All-Star Game. As much as we hated practice, that one was by far the best. We were playing football with legends. The kid in me wanted to run right up to players and ask for their autographs; the adult in me did. I didn't feel too bad, as I wasn't the only one to fill a football with autographs. In fact, every player was given their own football for just that purpose. We spent the rest of the day walking through the plays; of course we took numerous breaks to consume catered meals and sign autographs.

We practiced for two more days until it was game day. The All-Star Game was outside, so we were able to play right next to the ocean. The air was salty, warm, and full of excitement. When the game started, all the players seemed to have fun. Since it wasn't a real game, the score didn't matter much. The game was merely a celebration of being selected as an all-star and having fun was highly encouraged. I still wanted to take the opportunity to show the voters why I deserved to be on the first-team, though. When the ball was snapped, I pushed the offensive tackle from Arkansas out of my way. Within seconds, I was facemask-to-facemask with the quarterback from Anchorage. As we lied on the turf together, I had massive amounts of adrenaline flowing through my body after having earned my first sack as a Professional Football League All-Star. The adrenaline was quickly replaced by giddiness as reality set in; I was now nose-to-nose with one of the best quarterbacks of all times. I went from trash talking, to speechless, in no time flat.

A few hours later, the game was over. I don't remember who won that game, but I do remember how much fun we had. We hung out with a bunch of the players at the hotel that night, and flew home the next day. With the season officially over, we again had a few months to enjoy the off-season until we had to get ready for that next year. After the two of us winning the Offensive Player of the Year, the Defensive Player of the Year, the league's MVP, making it to an all-star game, going to the playoffs, breaking records, and leading the league in stats, who knew what the following season would bring?

Chapter 103

It didn't take long for us to find out our future. A few weeks after the all-star game, I received a call from the general manager. He wanted to talk to me in his office as soon as possible. I figured the manager wanted to talk to me about my new contract because I had clearly exceeded his expectations. Mike and I happened to be out golfing at the time, so after an embarrassing loss, he drove me to my meeting.

The general manager met me at his office door and asked me to sit right away. As we shook hands, something seemed different. The last time we met, he had really good news for me, which was reflected in his tone of voice. That time, however, his tone didn't seem to reflect good news; I wasn't really sure what it reflected.

He started the meeting congratulating me on making it to the all-star game, and for my achievements during the season. He was proud of my success, and knew I would only get better as a player. After crunching some numbers, he was able to come up with a contract that he knew I would enjoy, and one that would be a reflection of my worth to the team. Sadly, the contract was too pricy for the team, as they already had a high-priced running back.

The obvious solution to *me* was to reduce my salary. I knew I was making quite a bit of money as it was, so I wouldn't notice the difference between a big raise and the really big raise I expected. Instead, the business man in *him* came out. He had already made a deal with another team. He found a team in Wyoming that would accept me, and my new contract, and would give him two players, as well as an additional pick in the upcoming Selection

Showcase, in return. As he explained it, why have one expensive player when you can have two at the same price?

Although his reasoning was justifiable, it was still devastating. My parents lived in Michigan, my wife had a steady job she loved, we had our own home, I was very comfortable with the team, and I was playing football with my best friend. All of a sudden, I was penalized for an outstanding season and had to move to a new town without any input. I was no longer a person on the team; I was a contract on a desk. Even if I willingly packed up everything, said goodbye to my friends and family, and moved my wife and son to Wyoming, there would be no guarantee that I wouldn't be traded to another team the following season.

When I told Mike the news, he was just as shocked as I was. Not only was he upset for me, but he was also upset that I would be leaving after spending so many years trying to earn the right to play together. He was so outraged that he stormed into the general manager's office to tell him off. Mike reminded the manager that he was a big part of the team and the team was nothing without him. If they really did go through with the trade, he would have no choice but to walk away from the team. Other teams would certainly want him. Although it wasn't his plan, Mike wanted the Knights to know how important it was to him that I stayed. The manager took a few minutes to think about it, then gave him his decision. The general manager was surprisingly calm and stated, "Do you know how many players I could get for the price of your contract?"

Mike was crushed. He now felt what I felt. Even though he was their best athlete, in a matter of minutes, he was just another contract on a desk. Since they were willing to walk away from him, he was more than happy to walk away from them. He knew it wasn't just our team that treated players like numbers. He knew all teams did it, so he didn't even make an effort to find another team. In the heat of the moment, he retired from professional football after playing for only five years. After a few days of cooling down and thinking about his decision, he didn't regret it.

With Mike's retirement being official, and the threat of being shipped to Wyoming, I followed his lead. After discussing it with Christine, I also decided to retire. After spending two years in high school, four years in college, and four years in the pros, I had enough. I had to walk away from the sport that treated me so well, because of a manager that treated me so poorly. But there was no regret. We set a goal as juniors in high school, and we achieved the goal after much hard work and dedication. Collectively, we went through state championships, recruiting trips, scout teams, Selection Showcases, practice squads, declaring early for the pros, big contracts, little pay checks, injuries, and disappointment to make it to where we were; suddenly we were retiring in our mid-thirties with more money than we knew what to do with, and two-thirds of a lifetime ahead of us. No regrets.

Chapter 104

Mike and I both continued to live in Michigan. We lived in homes that were fully paid for, and enjoyed our new retired lives. For about a year, the two of us spent plenty of time together, as we had plenty of time to spare, and had many conversations about our playing days. In those conversations, we never questioned our decision to leave. We left at the peak of our playing careers, and were idolized in the papers for months after our decision. After a year, though, we began to live different lives.

We started getting bored at about the same time. There was only so much we could do with our free time and eventually, there was nothing left to do at all. I had a great wife and son, so at least I had my family to spend my time with. He wasn't so lucky, though. Early in his professional career, he chose not to get seriously involved with women because he simply didn't trust them with his money. Unfortunately, he felt he was too old to start looking for a serious relationship, he was no longer considered a sports hero, and he still felt that women only wanted him for his money. His sports friends had quit coming by and soon, Christine and I were the only real friends he had.

To make his life less isolated, he moved his parents into his home. They were getting older and he decided it was his time to care for them. He obviously had the money to support them, and he had the room to house them. Even with his parents there, though, his life still felt empty. He decided to use his talents find a job. He never received a college degree, and received poor grades in the three years he did spend in college. His only expertise was his knowledge of football. One of the local sports networks decided to pick him up as a sports analyst, but that job didn't pay very much. He did, however, love the job and stuck with it until he was ready to retire a second time.

Meanwhile, I also wanted to find a second career. I enjoyed my time as a security guard, so I chose to get back into the field. With the money I had, plus my college education in business, I was able to start my own security company. After a few very successful years, I was making more money from the business than I would have if I continued to play football. Once again, I had the wife of my dreams, a son that one could only wish for, and a job that I loved doing. Life was awesome.

I thought about our paths from time to time, Mike's and mine, and how different they were. As a high school player, Mike was one of the best. He was popular, and was recruited by several major colleges. After three years as a college student, he was selected as the number one pick by our favorite professional football team. He made a lot of money and, after only five years, was able to comfortably retire. Sadly, he still felt empty and had to move his parents in just for company. He didn't have much education, and could only get a job based on who he was.

On the other hand, it took me a long time to develop into a football player. It took so long that I had to play two years at the junior college level just to get noticed. After a year of backup duties, and a year of starting, I only had enough experience to make the scout team at a major college. I eventually made my way as a backup player on a national championship winning team. I went on to start the following year, only to disappoint the fans with a losing season. After only a year as a college starter, I was able to fight my way onto a professional football team, only to make the practice squad for two seasons. I eventually became an all-star, but only for a short time as I chose to walk away from football due to team politics. I walked right out of the challenging life of professional football, and right into my considerably more rewarding life of marriage, family, and business ownership. Although I wouldn't have changed a thing, and was glad that I made the life choices I did, when I think about our two paths, I still come to the same conclusion every time: Linemen have all the guts, but running backs still get all the glory.

Epilogue

I thought that when we retired from football that day, we would be walking away from it completely. However, after going through all of the frustration and excitement of a career in professional football, it was now fun watching Alan begin to walk in my footsteps. It's crazy to watch him create the same memories that I shared with my best friend many years ago. Today, Mike and I both coach youth football. And as much fun as I had playing on the field with him, I am having even more fun coaching against him. Although we left the game as athletes, we will forever stay in the game as fans.

Made in the USA
Lexington, KY
19 February 2018